## *WAR ON VASSA*

"*And the Thana. What about them? The Thana who would follow you anywhere, into anything, because they think you are a god.*" *Mirren's face was white.* "*Against the Vanth, backed by only three Litani, it was a struggle. But against twenty thousand—*"

"*Mirren, my love.*" *Brian, the great warrior, brushed her cheek gently with his fingers.* "*We cannot set the Thana, with their swords and arrows, against lasers, bo-blasters, and we don't know what else. They can only lose. It has to be between us and the newcomers.*"

*Mirren's patrician features were scored with worry.* "*It is not just the waiting. It is the doubting. Brian, what will the newcomers do when they find Soro, Rogo, and Woluf dead—by our hands?*"

*He shrugged.* "*It was them or us.*" *He picked up his bo-blaster, gripped it tightly in his big hand.* "*So now we negotiate—with this.*"

We will send you a free catalog on request. Any titles not in your local bookstore can be purchased by mail. Send the price of the book plus 50¢ shipping charge to Leisure Books, P.O. Box 511, Murray Hill Station, New York, N.Y. 10156—0511.

Titles currently in print are available for industrial and sales promotion at reduced rates. Address inquiries to Nordon Publications, Inc., Two Park Avenue, New York, N.Y. 10016, Attention: Premium Sales Department.

# FIRE THRONE MOUNTAIN

E. Rew Bixby

TOWER BOOKS   NEW YORK CITY

*For Pat and Jean.*

A TOWER BOOK

Published by

Tower Publications, Inc.
Two Park Avenue
New York, N.Y. 10016

Copyright © 1981 by Tower Publications, Inc.

All rights reserved
Printed in the United States

## one

Eckem Meluq might have grown there, fitting like a piece of wadding into the command chair of the orbiting space craft. Intently his colorless eyes watched the large comm screen before him, where the green blip showed the shuttle bearing Lazo Rataq and a hundred picked men dropping swiftly away toward the surface of Vassa.

Inwardly Meluq smiled, but nothing showed on his jowly face. Rataq and a hundred picked men—picked to be expendable. If the pre-advance party already on the planet were still able to guide Rataq into the land-launch tube, so much the better; they could get on with the off-loading. If the last frantic messages, then the long radio silence, meant the pre-advance was no longer functioning, then Lazo Rataq would be forced to expend all his fuel landing elsewhere without landside help. And then Lazo would have to lead a raid to capture the land-launch tube at Colufo. Or, if the people from Earth had learned to operate the magnetics, they might crash the shuttle to the ground the way Rogo had wrecked the Earth scout ships months ago. And if so, at least he was rid of Rataq and certain other undesirables.

Eckem Meluq rubbed his fat hands together and

adjusted the neck brace that helped support his bulbous head on his flabby neck. No matter what, to send in the shuttle with Rataq and that crew without delay was a wise decision. He interlaced his fingers, rested them on his massive belly and nodded in satisfaction.

Before another screen, on the ground, on Vassa itself, three persons sat close together in the couch chairs at the console of a scout ship control room. All eyes were locked on two green blips. The larger spot continued on its orbital path. The smaller had separated away and now drifted with agonizing slowness on the screen. Its path was the beginning of a long descending arc. They knew its end would be at the center of the display. That which they had long expected and greatly feared was coming to pass.

Brian Boru McCann broke into the tension. "Well, by Llu, here they come at last." He said it with a certain relief in his voice. "Soon we'll have action." He bounced his large frame up from the hi-g couch to pace back and forth from the seat to the open hatch. Two steps only, it was not enough in any way to relieve his tension. His once white one-piece uniform, scrounged from the wreck of the *Tsiolkovsky* and made for a smaller man, was split at the shoulders and strained across his chest. Unconsciously his strong right hand gripped the hilt of the sword hanging at his hip from a Thana harness buckled over the uniform. His craggy face and thin lips twisted into a grin at the anachronism of clutching at a sword when the threat was from spacers dropping down toward them in a shuttle. But then that sword—it had a name, Vanth Nugol—helped him carve his way through the Vanth into this control room of the grounded scout ship. Maybe it still would have meaning. His eyes flipped back to the moving dot on the radar screen.

"If I could carve those blips out of the screen with the point of my long sword and throw them away—that would do it, wouldn't it?" He picked up a boblaster from the console desk. "Or I could disintegrate the whole screen with this...." He laughed and dropped the blaster again. He felt tense as an armed missile with a hair trigger and the gunner's finger on the red button ready to twitch.

"Waiting is nearly over," Mirren Fitzgerald said, but her voice was taut as a stretched spring. Her close-cropped blonde head did not stir. Her attention was shackled to the display raster. Her long-fingered hands hovered over knobs and buttons that were labeled with strange characters, touching, micro-adjusting but making no significant change in the visual.

Their waiting endured in a Litanofoq scout ship that would never fly again. It now was a part of Colufo Castle, a round tower, a ship encased in rough gray stone.

"We just have to find a way to talk with them. To negotiate." Mirren was talking hope to herself in the face of utter failure.

Their mission was to verify information the probes had transmitted about the second planet orbiting Barnard's star. They indicated that it was eminently suitable for human colonization. The two ships of the scouting expedition, the *Goddard* and the *Tsiolkovsky,* carried a team of specialists and extensive instrumentation for analysis of planet conditions and the gathering of as much understanding of the planet as possible to make colonization safe and successful.

So great was the faith in the probe reports that following one year after the advance ships had cast off, the great transport *Plymouth* also lifted away from Earth orbiting station 024 with the first

10,000 colonists desperate to leave a radiation-poisoned earth.

Brian tugged impatiently at his short red beard. "Ngora, let's have a cup of dolagu. It is still ards before they arrive."

Ngora Goroga lifted her massive body ponderously from her console chair, black face a contrast above the white of her uniform, gold front tooth gleaming in her smile. "The last ard of waiting fires the greatest anxiety."

Brian glanced at her with his sharp blue eyes. "So how can you be so relaxed?"

"Worry is a damaging exercise. I try to avoid it."

"Quarks, only a frustrated doctor would say something like that."

Ngora slapped his shoulder lightly with the back of her hand. "Easy does it," she said, as she stepped down the metal grating spiral stairs toward the galley.

Brian gazed again at the radar display, letting out his breath in a rasping sigh. They were in a trap, on the knife edge of disaster. They all knew it. They had all accepted it, knowing it. And Brian was resigned to it—almost.

All those poor people fleeing earth and expecting. . . ." Mirren clenched her jaws against the nausea of despair. "What will they find here? And we have no way to warn them."

Brian felt the note of near hysteria in her voice. He stepped behind her to knead some relaxation into the back of her neck and shoulders with his great hands.

She let her head droop for the relaxing fingers, and other worries flooded in.

"And the Thana, what about them? The Thana who would follow you anywhere, into anything, because they think you are a god." Her face was a strained white but a brief light sparked in her blue eyes. "Because it was you, the headlong dash of you, the grand redheaded Irishman with the great muscles swinging a hand-forged sword. Oh, it was a great fighter you were, Brian Boru come to life again." Then the light faded. "Against the Vanth, backed by only three Litani, it was a struggle. But against twenty thousand...."

"Mirren, my love." He brushed her cheek gently with his fingers. "You know we cannot ever think of setting the Thana, with their swords and arrows, against lasers, bo-blasters and we don't know what else. They can only lose. It has to be between us and the newcomers."

Mirren swiveled her hi-g chair around to look up at Brian, her fair patrician face again dark with worry. "It is not just the waiting. It is the doubting. Brian, what will the newcomers do when they find that Soro, Rogo and Woluf are all dead and we killed them?"

Brian shrugged. "It exploded into them or us. Up there—" he nodded toward the comm screen— "they know a battle was going on here. So we negotiate. Negotiate from weakness." He picked up the bo-blaster, gripped it tight in his big hand, ground his teeth and threw it down again.

Mirren spoke rapidly, and Brian caught the strained tone of her voice. "We do have a card to play. And we don't know if it's an ace or a trey."

Brian's grin had no smile in it. A hundred times they had been over it. Why permanently ground a small space ship? They thought they knew: to use its power first to sink a long extending tube on a slant deep into the ground, a land-launch tube—it could be intended for no other use. And the ship was now its operating control center.

Mirren continued around the old circle of words again. "A hundred to one their mother ship cannot land at all. They must use shuttles. They are fuel short, after eons in space. They need the tube for both landing and launching. There is no mechanism for transporting a ship to the tube any way than to set down in it. And I can use their G&M. I can catch that descending ship and drop it into the tube, and pin it there while we find a way to talk to them." She banged on the console desk with her fist. "I believe I can do it. I know I can."

"That's the spirit, Mirren my dove. No, not my dove, my falcon, my eagle. I have seen you with the light of galaxies shining in the blue of your eyes, and there's the proud arch of the rainbow that reaches to the heavens in the line of your neck and your haughty chin, and the dauntless back of you straight and unbowed as the great spear of Finn McCoul himself. We stand and fight. Not with blasters but with wit and words."

She almost laughed. "Maybe the blarney can do it."

Brian's voice turned grim. "There's a problem we're leaving out in all this talk about talk: we don't know the language, even with all the radio we have listened to from that ship which was trying to contact Rogo or Soro."

"Still, you're the linguistic anthropologist of the expedition. I delegate the talking to you. I will hold that ship to give you your chance. You have to find a way to communicate or . . . or it's the end of everything." She stared at the moving spots on the display, with all those numbers. "Microsponder control again." Her hands clenched on the edge of the console desk, knuckles white. "I would rather be wiped out."

"Mirren, that transponder control inside your brain is burned out. It can't be operated again."

She looked up, her face white on white, showing the edges of fear. "The newcomers can implant another."

"Never!"

He lifted her, held her close, felt the tremor that fluttered through her body. He remembered the disintegration of her personality when all her thoughts and actions had been controlled, directed, by Litani from this console where she sat. No wonder the thought of again being commanded from inside her own brain, by aliens who implanted a control there, was frightening.

The Litani could easily perform another operation. They could do it to Ngora and Brian too! He crushed Mirren tightly against his chest.

Ngora clumped up the last steps with three mugs of steaming dolagu and saw their embrace. "Beautiful," she said. "Beautiful. Best thing in the world for the health of my patients. But if you want a sip while the dolagu is hot you have to break it up."

With the tang of the steam rising in his nostrils, Brian gazed over the rim of his mug at the slowly moving spot of light and listened to the highpitched voices coming over the monitor speaker. That talk had to be the comm talk between the approaching shuttle and the orbiting ship. Brian had been listening to those occasional bursts of speech on that monitor for five months now as the signals grew gradually stronger, but with all his listening he had not been able to learn enough language to be of any real significance. He had made no attempt to talk, just listened. Any try at talking would have betrayed his position.

Now he heard messages spoken to someone called Rataq; answers were addressed to an Eckem Meluq. Rataq must be on the shuttle, because the signals remained clear and grew stronger, while the others faded as the orbit carried the mother ship around the planet.

"Colufo, Colufo. If anyone is there, answer on channel RQ." The monitor crackled with the words. "*Colufo, Colufo.* If anyone is there, answer on channel RQ."

"My God!" Mirren's mouth flopped open. "They are speaking Earth basic."

Brian searched for an explanation. "Rogo may have sent reports of what they learned in your mind when they had you under control—enough to learn language, maybe total recordings."

"But all these months they have been approaching, they never used Earth before."

Brian felt a great elation. "We get our chance! They are going to ask for help in landing."

Their eyes met as Mirren reached to open the channel. She was all business now, with a gleam of hope in her eyes. "*Colufo* here, *Colufo* here," she called.

"Good. Good," came the answer. "Where are our men, Rogo, Soro or Woluf?"

Mirren answered in a totally neutral voice. "They are not available."

"Can you vector us in?"

"Yes." Mirren crossed her fingers. "Be there, terminal control," she muttered, and switched. The label on the knob read $\zeta \lambda \xi$.

The screen transformed instantly to a dimly glowing cube. Within it shone a central solid-line descent path, and dashed cursor lines for operational limits. The curved cursors widened through the cube from bottom left to top right, a bending inverted cone surrounding the central parabolic arc, a cone to catch a ship coasting with vectors of residual forward drift from orbital motion and vertical drop of rate of descent.

A moving blip glimmered above and behind the cone, top right.

Mirren jerked erect. She rolled the track ball under her fingers, swung the cone under the blip. Still it kept drifting away across the cube.

"Reduce thrust! Reduce thrust! Increase descent rate," she called.

The spot of light dropped toward the edge of the cone and traveled on the edge of the dashed cursor.

"Reduce thrust again. Slowly, slowly." The blip coasted through the line into the cone.

"Got you!" she said. "Got you."

"Are we in the horn?" asked a voice.

"You are in the horn."

"Then turn on Tusagra."

"Turn on what?"

"Tusagra."

Her voice rose in pitch. "I don't know how."

Words burst quickly from the screen. "Switch to channel RX."

Mirren switched. The screen blanked, then, instantly, the finger of a hand wrote in glowing letters $\gamma \varsigma \psi \mu$. She found the labeled switch and flipped it, then returned the screen to the former display. "It's the M&G's," she said. "I should have known."

Colored green lines of force leaped out to the spot of light, enveloped it. Mirren adjusted the knob to see if she could control the motion. The lines faded thinner; the ship dropped faster. She reversed the twist; the lines thickened, the ship slowed. She said, "If I turned the M&G's off now that ship would just drop." Her hand hovered over the knob, her face intent on the screen. "There's a feeling, almost like piloting again. I wish. . . ."

A tense but controlled voice spoke. "Better switch to automatic. Manual guidance is difficult for a first-time landing." The man was worried.

Mirren whispered, "If I put them on auto, I can't hold them for negotiation. If I keep it on manual, I could mess it up."

"Automatic into the tube, then back to manual," Brian said quickly.

Mirren nodded. "Right."

Brian's teeth ached from the pressure. He rubbed his jaw, pulled at his red beard.

The green lines slowly cushioned the spot of light that was the ship and then more slowly guided it down the cursor line toward the land-launch tube.

"Do you have your reception speech ready?" Mirren asked brightly.

## two

Mirren flipped again the switch marked γ ς ψ μ. Now they gazed into a command and control room similar, except that it was larger, to the cramped quarters in which they sat. Four men stared back at them, three of them short and stocky but the fourth taller and slighter in build. All their faces were roundish and black. The eyes of three were hooded and somber, but the eyes of the taller one flamed with life. He must be Rataq, Brian thought, and examined him closely. The low bridge of the nose, the rounded forehead and face suggested youth, even childishness, but the crinkled black skin and the firm, well-defined line of jaw and chin said maturity. The intense eyes that burned out from under the curve of forehead said intelligence, purpose and drive. From a bright metal chain around his neck hung a heavy jewel, large, green and held in a complex setting. Rataq's hand reached up to finger it. All wore similar uniforms, silver in color, metallic in texture. Only Lazo Rataq wore a jewel. They all seemed fit and alert, their movements quick and sure, ready for anything.

Brian cleared his throat, but Rataq spoke first. "Three of you," he said. "Tall man, fair skin, red hair and beard: Brian McCann. A black woman, tall, large boned: Ngora Goroga. And another woman, slender, fair skin, yellow hair: Mirren Fitzgerald. You see, I know you all. Our scout's messages came in great detail. Interesting—you three must represent two, or maybe three, of the great families of Earth. And where are our scouts?"

Brian smiled a strained smile. "Well, they are not here . . . now."

Rataq waved his hand in a dismissing gesture. "Later," he said, and went swiftly on, his voice eager, excited. "I watched through a port coming in—green fields, prairies extending on and on, broad rivers, gray ocean, red clouds, dark green forests; beautiful. I must get out to see all these things close by. All of them I have seen, of course, on our micro readers, but never had I thought they were so beautiful. The reader spoke of the touch of spring breezes carrying the fragrance of wild flowers. I must get into the fields to touch, to feel, to smell that fragrance. This is our ancient home, you know, the one we left generations, many generations ago, when it was all poisoned. But now it seems much like it was before, as shown in our pictures." He paused. "There is delay in dropping up to exit level. Can I assist you?"

Brian was puzzled. Either this Rataq was a great actor developing a wily ambush or he really was as naive as he sounded, unconscious of the potential for conflict. "Before you come out of the ship, we would like to have some understanding," Rataq said.

"Oh, you want to know about landing your people when they arrive." Brian spread his arms in a wide gesture. "The planet is large. Plenty of empty space. They can land many places. Around on the other side, perhaps."

"Then you will help us to select a good spot for

them. We have no transportation except for the local animals."

"Of course, to be sure, that is a good idea. When our air cars are brought down, you can use one to search out good places, and we will be about our business here. This lander-launcher system seems to be operating well except just getting to the exit level. Is there a control problem?"

It was all too easy, Brian thought. But the way he slipped in the probing knife of a question without any change of expression at the end of each statement, he knows what he is doing. It smelled more and more of a trap. "What assurance do we have that your goal, as ours, is for peace?"

"Yes," Rataq said easily, "you are right to worry about releasing us. We could overwhelm you. Just four of us here in the command room, but there are a hundred more on the ship. Let me tell you about us; somewhere you may find your assurance." He paused in thought, then began slowly at first, reflectively.

"Long ago a horrible war was fought on this planet. In order to live our ancestors fled in many space ships. Maybe some of them found suitable worlds; I hope so. Perhaps one of them was your Earth. We do not know what happened to any of the other ships, but in many ways you seem very similar to us.

"Our ship, Foqal, found no livable planet anywhere in the curve of space. We have returned to find that Vassa is again hospitable. We find also that others managed to remain alive here, although they are much changed. The Thana, for instance, our scouts told us—will they be available soon? The Thana lived underground for many generations and developed infrared eyes for seeing in the dark, fur for warmth in the ever-present cold of the caves. And now we find you people who have traveled here through space. You also have a sophisticated technology. If your race and ours should contest for the exclusive use of this planet, it seems to me very probable that we would again poison the land and the water, and the atmosphere. Those of us left would again be forced to flee into cold empty space. We need this planet. We cannot allow this to happen."

He leaned forward and his voice quickened. The burning intensity of his dark eyes lanced fiercely at the three watching the video. It was not possible to doubt him. "We long to live again, as did the ancients, in the open, under the sky, with the daytime sun and the nighttime stars, and the changing seasons of the year. We yearn for it, crave it, reach for it as a man dying of thirst reaches for water. These are things on which we have dreamed all our lives and our fathers before us, but have seen only on our readers. We have never felt the warmth of the sun, the wet of the rain, the cold of the snow. Do you have all these on Earth?"

His face relaxed to an almost dreamy look.

"How is it on Vassa? What are the smells of the forest, the growing grass, the brown dirt? What is the sound of insects in the evening, of birds singing at dawn? The sight of a field of grain waving in a breeze, a sunlit glade deep in the woods, a mirror lake under a snowcapped mountain with pink clouds floating? What is the taste of bread made from thalis or loggets ground from the golden grain? What is the taste of milk from the mesors and of meat from animals that live in field and forest?"

He paused, his dream faded, his face grew sad. "All our food is recycled waste. Even though we use certain plants as a portion of our process and add energy, still basically it is all recycled waste.

Our air is recycled, and the scrubbers can never eliminate all the smells of the many-times-used air, the sweetness of sweat, the sour of flatulence. We live in the constraints of a totally closed loop; nothing may be allowed to escape. Everything must be reprocessed carefully, completely.

"And yet some of us, while they crave the freedom of the planet, also fear the change. All their lives and for many generations before, reaching back to the beginning of the trip, we have lived close together in tiny rooms bounded by metal walls. The only space we knew was the deadly space beyond the skin of the ship. Some of us are desperately afraid of being outside the womb of the walls. And of course we are accustomed to the noises: many people close together in the ship, the blowers—always the drone of blowers sucking air. Without the circulation, our poisons would accumulate in stagnant corners. Some of us will be fearful of silence. But these people also need living room, even though they may cling to complexes like the one under Colufo Castle. No progress has been reported on it for six months." He stopped, waiting for an answer.

Brian felt the pressure of the piercing eyes, but stubbornly he remained silent.

Finally Rataq resumed. "If there is insufficient space at Colufo we will take over certain caves of which you know." Brian opened his mouth to speak.

"Now be patient." Rataq waved his hand.

One of Mirren's pet phrases, Brian thought. He sounds like Mirren giving a lecture.

"Living thus, crowded and close, our custom has become always to defer to one another. In our living conditions, it was necessary. Arguments, competition, passions, angers, aggression, all have been nearly squeezed out of two of our great families. Otherwise how could the many generations have lived together in our ship? This is true for all but the one ruling family. It was needful to have strong leadership, so one family and its descendants are permitted strong feelings, drive, ambition, enough of the aggressive qualities to control. Otherwise even a people trained to non-aggression could not have existed over the eons. Disorganization would have destroyed us, lack of positive assignment of duties, the force to ensure the duties were carried out. And some duties are grim.

"Our ship is filled to capacity, has always been so. There is no room for additions, neither could our life-support systems care for any more. Therefore we practice rigid birth control to maintain a no-growth population. If by miscalculation some babe is born during a time period when there is no matching death of an aged one, then a death is necessary—either an aged volunteer or the babe. That is our law. The adults have choice, the babe has none. It is a bitter decision.

"There are many pregnant females on our ship. They hope for a world where limitation of population will no longer be required. We must have peace for our children. And we must not poison this planet again."

He was silent. His fierce eyes bored into the watchers.

"Now do you understand that we will do all in our power to live with you in peace?"

Rataq leaned back straight and proud in his command chair. "Also I am eckem—Master—on Vassa. Events will take place here as I command." Then he added as a forced afterthought, "I am eckem, at least, until Eckem Meluq shall descend to us."

Brian looked at Mirren, at Ngora. They all

nodded.

Brian and Ngora used a gravy boat—a circular antigravity plate with a handle-like structure rising on one side for control and a center post for riders to steady themselves—to drop down a vertical shaft to the first shuttle-exit level. They walked swiftly along the black glass-lined corridor to the heavy double doors that sealed the corridor from the slanting land-launch shaft.

As they approached the doors were flung open before them, and Rataq, with his three companions, marched through, all in close-fitting silver uniforms. Behind them Brian could see into the command and control room.

A voice boomed from the comm speakers in the ship, giving commands in Foq language. Then the voice switched to Earth common. "Now hear this. Now hear this. This is Eckem Meluq speaking. There is no eckem but Meluq. There is no eckem but Meluq. Terko Ubeq is now in ground command on Vassa. He will seize Lazo Rataq and the Earth people at once." He barked more orders in Litanofoq. Then in Earth he sneered, "Lazo Rataq is not the only one who can learn Earth language." His laughter echoed down the hall.

At the words, everyone froze: Rataq, the three men following him, Brian and Ngora.

Rataq jerked around to stare with flinty eyes at the man behind him. "You!"

The grin on Terko Ubeq's round face, with its drooping mustache, was insolent and malicious.

Brian was trying to draw his sword, but he saw Ubeq pulling a blaster from his hip holster and knew he did not have time. Brian dove headlong past Rataq and rolled into the legs of Ubeq.

A blaster shot crackled over him into the floor beyond. Brian's roll tumbled Ubeq into the men behind and they all fell in a tangle. Ngora jumped to lift the top Litani from the heap. Rataq recovered the blaster that Ubeq had dropped. Ngora snatched two more blasters as the Litani untangled.

Brian jumped up with his eyes on Lazo Rataq. It was a trap, he thought, but was Rataq caught in it, or was he running it?

"Thanks," Rataq said. He stared into Brian's eyes for a moment, looked away. "Sometimes it is hard to know allies from enemies."

Ngora called, "More coming!"

Brian wheeled around past the three Litani lined against the wall under two-gun Ngora's blasters. Beyond the corridor doors and the shuttle hatch, more Litanofoq were appearing in the command room around the corner from a passageway, and starting toward them on the run.

The ship's doors snapped shut.

Brian relaxed. Mirren is on the ball up there, he thought. He turned back to Rataq. "That will hold them for awhile."

Rataq shook his head. "Ship's controls can override that magnetic control. The hatch on the lower level opened at the same time as this one. Our men will soon be here; we have only a few moments. They heard Eckem Meluq too."

It was time to run, but a thought popped into Brian's mind. "Could you have dropped your ship to the exit level?"

"Yes." Rataq smiled. "But I wished to talk with you." He put the prime question to Brian. "You agree that there is room on the planet for both our people?"

Brian answered quickly, "Our planet has had its devastating wars. We want peace on this planet. We agree." He held out his hand. "Shake."

Rataq seemed puzzled, then he extended his hand hesitantly. "Your custom?"

"Our custom." Brian gripped once. "Now run."

## three

Alone in the command room of the orbiting ship, Eckem Meluq glared at the shifty-eyed round face of Terko Ubeq on his comm screen. He leaned forward slightly in his command chair and watched Terko's stocky body shrink back. Meluq felt the extent of his power; it was effective even from a thousand obu away. Even in his anger he gloated a bit. He kept his voice soft, but it hissed like a snake.

"You let Rataq escape, and all you can think of is to come whining to me to send down an air car! You have technicians down there. Get some implants into Thana heads so you can control them, then get them out searching. Get those Earthians, too. Why do you think we developed zotoradiation control? Make Zotors!"

Meluq eyed Terko's blank expression. Snubnosed idiot, he thought. I need some competents down there, but I had to send expendables the first trip; can't be reckless with the good brains.

The slits of Terko's pale eyes avoided Meluq's gaze. "It will take time. We have only one small operating room," he complained.

Meluq's dark puffy face was turning purple, his fat earlobes glowed. "So keep it working," he exploded. "All day, all night. Do you have a technician operating there now? Do you have a string of Thana waiting?"

"Well, uh . . . uh. . ."

"I thought not. Jet to it or you will not be ground commander for long." He flipped the cutoff switch on the control panel beside the chair arm, muttering, "Only long enough to get the next shuttle down there."

Another switch flashed a different scene before him: Litanofoq, all carrying bundles like a scurrying string of harvester ants, trotting along the dull gray metal-walled passageway toward the airlock entrance to the second shuttle.

His fingers pressed up another scene, the command and control room of that shuttle, crowded with bays and consoles of equipment, its hi-g chairs, and the crew. Meluq zoomed in on Barsorq in the No. 1 chair: deep-lined rumpled face, sharp nose jutting out in a tight curve from its low bridge.

"How soon do you drop off?"

Barsorq glanced up at the digital time display atop the navigation console. "At 11:50 hours exactly."

Meluq nodded. "Good. When you arrive groundside, relieve Terko Ubeq of command. Put him to work fulltime zotoing Thana and finding Rataq. Drive him. Drive him hard. Hammer him. Get full control of this planet before that ship arrives."


The Thana call their planet Vassa, the second planet from its sun that the Thana call yann. Earthians call it Barnard's star. Vassa is smaller than the sun and cooler, 3000 degrees Kelvin to the sun's 5800 degrees. Orange to red in color, it radiates less heat and light than the sun, and the spectral energy distribution of that light peaks in the red and infrared wavelengths instead of the blue area. But Vassa is much closer to yann than Earth is to the sun, so that the energy received per square meter at its surface is in a similar range.

It was such early estimates, communicated back to Earth as scout ships first orbited Vassa—along with other conditions not too dissimilar, a year of eight and half Earth months, a day of 18 hours, a gravity of 1.2—that started the *Plymouth*, with its colonists, on its way toward Vassa before the scout ships had landed . . . and crashed in landing.

At midmorning the five—Rataq, Brian, Mirren, Ngora and their guide, Kors—entered the notch between towering red cliffs—Alward Janīr, the Red Gate, it was called, the only easy passage to the high plateau. Mounted on grybins that looked like shortlegged antelope cut off below the knees, they rode single file at a stiff trot up the canyon.

They were four days' ride from Colufo, and now the climb grew steeper. The trot was a jarring pace. The backs of the stumpy animals were too broad to grip well with the thighs, and the Thana had not developed stirrups. A grybin's short neck, instead of rising before the rider, giving some small sense of security, stretched forward at the same level as the body. The only upward extensions were the twin horns rising straight from the top of the forehead, then curving forward, but they were a false hope to use as a handle. Feeling a grip on a horn, a grybin immediately forgot everything else in the world except getting rid of the hold—bucking, stumbling, falling. Already Rataq was bruised from learning about using horns for a handhold.

For eleven kilometers the sand strip wound between its red sandstone walls—sometimes wide, with space for low green growth at the edges and an occasional stunted tree; sometimes narrow, nothing but wall-to-wall sand with a ruddy tinge—and always it climbed. During the big wet, for several months of the year, an impassable flood poured down the ravine; in the hot dry, nothing. But now, between the wet and the dry, a trickle meandered from side to side in the level spots and dripped down over bare red rocks where it was steep. Here they dismounted to lead scrambling slipping mounts up the way. The big sun, always as red as Earth sun at sunset, hung like a burning disc, pouring waves of heat that reflected down from red cliffs onto the riders.

Brian, at the rear, his saddle hardly more than a pad with a strap under the grybin's chest, jounced to the rhythm of his mount. He twisted around occasionally to peer behind them. Even though he did not like the closed-in feeling between the red walls, he had no worries. So far he had detected no pursuit; the frustrating inactivity of waiting was over, an interim of traveling meant a release from tension.

First they had fled to Tsankta to consult with Tavita and her husbands, Kors and Cogbard. They all had worried about where to hide. No matter how well concealed, they were sure Thana zotors would smell them out.

Kors had an idea. "To hide grain of sand, place it on the beach; to hide a blade of grass, drop it on the turf. On the steppe we will be just a few more nomads riding among the herds."

They left the same night for the high plateau, with Kors as a guide.

Ahead of him, Brian watched Mirren's straight proud back sway gracefully to the pace. She still looked cool in her fitted white uniform; her short golden hair shone in the sunlight. Beyond her, Ngora's massive body crushed down on her saddle, absorbing the jolts with no relieving motion.

The three of them were all who remained of the eighteen sent on the scouting expedition to the planets of Barnard's star. Instead of analyzing planet resources to give colonizing families—10,000 people—a quick jump toward self-sufficiency, the best they would hope to do—if they could do anything at all—was save them from the crash landings that had destroyed their scout ship. And they were running, but they had a key. With Lazo Rataq they had the possibility of success.

Brian looked ahead to Rataq, bobbing on his mount. His riding was improving, he had fallen sprawling in the sand only once today. And no wonder he had trouble. He had never ridden anything before, was too short to get any grip with his knees, and had nothing to hang onto. But he has guts, Brian thought; he won't give up. I'll make some stirrups first chance. We could all use stirrups.

Riding felt good: the trotting grybin under him, the splashing of hooves in the shallow stream, the clean dry air of the altitude. The only problem was the heat that sucked up his oozing sweat.

They were going to relax among the nomads for about a month, then Rataq would get in touch with his people. By that time they should all have disembarked from his ship. Then they would overthrow Eckem Meluq and his agent Ubeq. Cogbard was to follow them in three to four weeks to give them the situation as the Thana saw it.

So what if there were too many unknowns? They would take care of them as they came up. Brian hummed a tune to himself.

At the front of the file, Kors rode smoothly, wearing only his leather harness, wide belt with one shoulder strap supporting a sword and a knife, his bow and quiver tied to the saddle pad. Brian was accustomed now to the native Thana, with the cream-colored fur on their bodies and black fur on forearms and hands, below the knees and on their faces and heads; their pert catlike ears, their enormous multifaceted yellow eyes, the loose folds of skin they could lower from their brows and raise from their cheekbones to hood their eyes. Mirren, Ngora and Rataq, with hairless skin and ordinary eyes, seemed the strange ones now.

There is the problem, Brian thought, of locating and establishing relations with the nomads. Kors admits he has had no contact with the Thana-Kovas, the wanderers of the steppes, for many years, and he describes them as prideful, independent, unpredictable, jealous of the territory and suspicious of strangers. But that was Kors' problem. He would take care of it.

The red walls closed in, narrowing the white strip of sand. Rounding a corner in late afternoon, they came on the source of the stream—a spring gushing from the base of the cliff, forming a pool fringed by green shrubs. Moist air cooled sunburnt skin.

Rataq carefully, stiffly, slid from his grybin, knelt and drank directly from the cold water of the pool. He raised his head to speak in Thana. "That is better. The water in your leather bottles is worse than our water on the ship—different, but worse."

He grimaced and groaned as he unbent to stand again. "You say these nomads live on grybin back." He shuddered and kneaded with his fingers at the inside of one thigh. "I do not see how they can do it, not on these beasts. Our images of old days showed longer legged, more graceful animals than these. Riders enjoyed their motion. I had looked forward to a thrill in bestriding a grybin and racing the wind. But this!" Rataq jerked the reins harder than necessary to keep his grybin from wading into the pool.

Kors chuckled. "The soreness leaves after few

dhols."

"When I get control, I'll never sit on another grybin. And is this trip really necessary? Could we not have found some hiding place without this torture?"

Mirren squatted to fill her leather canteen. "You vetoed the caves," she said, "and the forest."

"Yes." Rataq sighed. "The nonadapters, the ones who are not able to stomach the open, will take over those caves, and the forest will be full of them rushing in fright to get there. But I thought we might have hidden at Castle Tsankta."

"First place a controlled Thana would look for us." Brian was holding back the grybins from fouling the pool until Mirren and Ngora had finished. "You said Ubeq would be making zotos as fast as his technicians could implant the transponders." Brian caught Mirren's eye as he said it.

She shook her head sadly. "All those poor Thana! There has to be a way to stop that."

Rataq glared; his hand reached for his jewel. "How can we colonize this place without workers who know the planet?"

Mirren caught her breath. The pupils of her eyes closed down to pinpoints, her cheeks blanched.

Brian changed the subject. "Kors," he said loudly, "you told us the Kiyatagu is one tribe among the many tribes of the Thana-Kovas. How will we find these Kiyatagu?"

Kors grinned, teeth showing white against the dark of his lips. "They find us. They find us soon. And make no moves with that, or that." He pointed at the blaster Brian wore on one hip and at the sword he wore on the other.

"You mean they guard this canyon?"

"They do. This is their territory."

"We could be ambushed."

"We could."

All four gazed at Kors with awareness growing in their eyes.

Mirren broke the silence. "But we come looking for safety. Up on the steppe we can disappear among the tribes, you said."

Kors stretched his tired back and shoulders. "I think they talk before they decide. You are strange. They are curious."

"But the risk! We are at their mercy."

Kors shrugged. "What is done without risk? I was blood brother to Benjak, leader of the Kiyatagu, but that was long ago. Now?" He finished with another shrug.

When they left the pool the sun no longer shone into the ravine, and a cold wind gusted down the venturi shape of the canyon. It was steep now and more rocky than sandy. They moved at a walk, grybins picking their footing step by step. Brian wished that the power pak for his uniform was not totally dead and long abandoned.

As they rounded a corner of the narrowing twisting ravine, they met a frightened chladni racing toward them. A kangaroolike animal half the size of the grybins, it hesitated an instant, terrified great eyes searching for a clear path. Then it came on with the desperate speed of panic. One great bound carried it over the heads of Kors and Rataq to land beside Ngora. It touched down on two great feet and the clublike fist of its single front limb. A second bound took it clear over Mirren and Brian. It twisted in the air, landed nearly at right angles to where it had been, and fled past the corner.

Rataq sat still in his saddle, eyes following the flight. "What a strange animal!" His face shone with delight.

Brian kicked his grybin past the others up to Kors. "Something ahead frightened that animal.

You think the ones we seek are waiting for us, hiding and waiting?"

"Possibly."

They proceeded, watchful and edgy.

Behind them, Rataq asked, "How do these Thana-Kovas live?"

"They follow grass," Kors answered. "When the weather is bad they stay in the river valleys out of the wind, under trees."

Rataq objected, "Soon Ubeq will be looking for us from air cars. There can be no hiding from air cars on the plains you describe."

"There's always wind—sometimes hot, sometimes cold, but always wind," Kors said. "They always wear cloaks with hoods. You'll look like everybody else. And if you're attacked, there are no better fighting men on Vassa."

From above a lance flashed down into the sand before Kors. It stood nearly erect, vibrating gently for a long moment, and then was still.

All eyes darted upward to search the rim, which now was not far above. There was no sign.

Brian half drew his blaster. "What now?"

"I told you they'd find us," Kors said. "Sit still. By the wobargu tails on the lance I know it is Kiyatagu."

Silently, all sound of hooves muffled in the sand, three Thana-Kovas on magnificent clean-limbed grybins appeared before them from around a great rocky pile. Each man had a short reflex bow with an arrow nocked on the string, held easily but ready to raise and fire in one fast motion.

The Kovas were larger than Kors, bigboned, heavier in build. Their mounts were taller than the lowland grybins. Their heads were raised, eyes alert; their horns stood higher and arched farther forward at the tips. Their coats were paler and thicker, and on the light gray of the rumps were handsome black stripes.

"Beautiful," Rataq breathed. "That is what we saw on our imagicon."

The two groups eyed each other during a long silence. Brian noted stern faces, their black fur grayed by weather and the dust of the open steppe. The muscles of their heavy brows and prominent cheeks pulled flaps of skin from above and below so that their great eyes peered through narrow slits on either side of flat noses. He noted too that there was black fur on their hands and feet, where they extended from their loose leather cloaks, held closed by the typical Thana harness, a belt around the waist supported by a heavy strap over one shoulder. A quiver of arrows hung on each one's hip and a sword on the other.

The grayed black faces gazed expressionlessly. The wings of their nostrils quivered, sniffing. Brian fingered his blaster, looked again toward the rim. He saw twenty Thana-Kovas, standing with arrows ready.

Kors held up both hands, empty.

"Who are you?" The call was harsh, rasping from the one in the center of the trio.

"Kors Forstane an Tsankta, blood brother to Benjak, deitch of Kiyatagu." He dropped his hands to his sides.

"What do you do here?"

"I came to find the Kiyatagu."

"Why do you seek the Kiyatagu?"

"I came to see Benjak, my ordon, my blood brother."

"Why do you hunt for Benjak?"

Kors straightened his back, sat tall on his grybin. "Does one need a reason to seek his ordon? Is not a blood brother like an arrow to his ordon's bow? Is not a blood brother like a sword to his hand? There is no need to look for a reason for one to seek his ordon."

A stillness fell, thick and unmoving. Above, the Kovas on the rim were dark statues against the bright sky.

Brian watched the faces of the three—lean, hard, weathered. Their bows were still resting in alert hands on the withers of their mounts. He licked his dry lips. His hand rested close to his blaster.

"Who are these?" the middle one asked, his face hard, his air dominating, as he waved past Kors toward the rest of the group.

"They are ones from the sky, from the great god Llu, who helped free us from Vanth—except the small one."

"And he?"

He is a newcomer, also from the sky."

The one who questioned tucked his bow beside his quiver, kicked his grybin, and advanced slowly.

He sat taller than the others, with heavily muscled forearms reaching out from his cape. His square jaw made his face rectangular. The other faces were triangular, broad at the top for their great eyes, but the jaws were narrow.

"Little eyes," he said, drawing close. "White skin and no fur. A white one and a black one. And this one, no fur but long red hairs on his chin." He gripped Brian's beard.

Brian grasped the hand that held his whiskers. They stared eye to eye.

Brian saw in the bulging yellow eyes the pattern of tiny dark lines, each pinpoint a micro eye. Thousands. In spite of having lived for six months with Thana, he still could see nothing in them, could grasp no message from such eyes. He had to watch the rest of the face, the heavy drooping brows, the cheek muscles below the eyes, the lips, the wings of the nostrils. Especially the wings of the nostrils.

The Kiyatagu dropped the covering skin folds from his eyes and moved his head in the small circles that meant he was examining closely, passing the image of Brian's face across the edges of his eye facets. His hand still held the beard. "Llu means nothing here. He has no power. We are guided by Nalpur of Runn, the sacred warrior king."

Brian's strong grip crushed down on the hand. They stared. Tension grew brittle.

"And just who in the cosmic black are you?" Brian said it softly, but in the stillness it seemed overloud.

"I am one who drives arrows through the hearts of my enemies. I am one who has split many Thana and many Vanth from skull to navel with this sword." He grasped the hilt. "I am Inibek Kob." His thin lips broke into a smile. "But by your beard of red, and the strength of your right hand, I think I would rather call you friend."

Brian released the hand. Inibek made a fist and cuffed him on the shoulder.

"Strong man. I like you. Like your women too." He was gazing at Ngora. "Smooth black skin shining like the sacred dark rock of Runn." He guided his mount toward her, brushed her cheek with his fingers, while she sat rigid in her saddle.

He urged his mount ahead a few steps, then whirled. "I am Inibek Kob, first companion to Benjak, yet never have I heard of Kors Forstane an Tsankta. We will go to Benjak. We will see."

## four

Before their track left the canyon, each Kiyatagu leaned down from his grybin to pluck up a fist-sized water-smoothed stone. At Kors' gesture, Brian and the others did likewise, except they dismounted and remounted.

"It is a 'thank you' to the spirit of the canyon for a safe passage," Kors said. "Flash floods have drowned Kovas in that canyon."

As they reached the tip of the ravine where it opened out onto the plain, each tossed his rock on a mound of stones beside the track with the muttered words, "Khandro shurupur."

Inibek waved ten of his men to stay and maintain watch on the canyon path. The rest moved on into the steppe.

Brian halted his grybin as he came fully out onto the high plateau. Before them spread grassy flat plains rolling like seas, one upon the other to the horizon. The greens of the grass were surging constantly, standing gray green, but swept by the wind, breaking into multitudes of shining drops, white caps on the seas, long grasses tossed into churning waves by a wind that had touched nothing else for a thousand kilometers. Now it wailed about his ears, cold, menacing.

They rode for ards, cleaving through grasses that reached to their ankles as they sat their mounts, and as they rode, Brian looked well at the grybins of these Kiyatagu. It was only Inibek Kob and his two lieutenants who rode the high-quality mounts. The rest of the grybins were like the lowland animals, shaggier, leaner, better conditioned, but with the same thick neck, low-hanging head and stumpy legs.

But Inibek's grybin loped with a free and easy motion, a steed born of the wind. It was formed with lines of true beauty, sleek gray coat with greenish tints and dark stripes rounding the hindquarters, broad forehead supporting the ribbed horns, rising like twin periscopes beside the long, alert, ever-moving, expressive ears. The face tapered from the great round eyes, protected by projecting brows and extra folds of skin, to the flaring nostrils, soft muzzle and mobile lips. It was the loveliest animal Brian had seen on Vassa, where most seemed stocky, squat, clumsy.

Beside him he heard Rataq mutter to himself, "A grybin like that I could ride—I *will* ride. I shall have one."

In the west, yann, the sun of Vassa, hung low, a blood-red circle on the horizon. Brian shivered. The wind had turned icy. He drew his leather cape tight about his body and its attached hood tight about his face. Mentally he complimented Kors for his forethought in bringing the packets of saad to trade for the Kiyatagu cloaks. He wondered if the five without cloaks regretted the trade. The dried saad leaves were the only thing the Thana-Kovas greatly desired but did not produce for themselves, since the bushes grew only in the lowland valleys far from their high country. Kors said that the leaves, chewed slowly and held in the cheek, brought relaxing euphoria and heroic dreams.

When they traded, Brian noted that each Kovas extracted his long pinned shoulder clasp, set with rough-cut jewels, from the leather. He asked how much for a brooch. They refused to sell at any price. "There are thorn bushes. We will get you long curved thorns to hold your cloaks."

That night they camped on the high plain, the center of the world. Grassland stretched in all directions to meet the rim of the great enclosing bowls of the sky. The land was big, the sky was enormous. Only the men, scraping a circle bare of grass for a fire, were small.

Over the glowing heat of dried magli and tipula dung, they barbecued the haunch and loin of a chladni that they had startled up from the grass during the afternoon. Inibek shot on its third jump, drawing his bow from its case, stringing it, nocking the arrow and shooting, all while his grybin, guided by his knees, sprang from walk to gallop in pursuit.

As they sat close around the fire, tired and content, gnawing the last bits of savory meat from the bones, Inibek Kob's Kel-Birat, neither tethered nor hobbled as the other mounts were, ambled up behind him, nuzzled the back of his neck, lipped his ear. Inibek reached up to pat the side of its neck and half rose to position the animal behind him, where it dropped to its knees, then all the way down, with its legs tucked under. Inibek sat again, leaning his back against the soft warm flank, sighed in comfort and scratched Kel-Birat's throat under its chin. The grybin stretched its neck, outthrust its muzzle in appreciation.

Rataq moved over to stroke the fur on the side of Kel-Birat's jaw. "Are there many such grybins on the steppe?"

"A few only, just one pure blood line, a gift from the gods given to the Kovas in the days of the beginning. Praise be to Nalpur, the Beneficent, the Merciful Warrior who strikes terror to the enemies of Runn."

"How may one acquire such an animal?"

"None ever are sold. By theft, by war or by gift."

Rataq patted Kel-Birat gently on the neck, speaking softly to himself. "By theft, war or gift. One day soon. . . ."

Brian gazed up at the black velvet curtain of sky that dominated this grass world. He knew how far away were the clean bright stars, yet they seemed close, like holes punched in the curtain that he could reach out and touch.

Inibek followed his gaze. "Those holes that let the white light through were jabbed through the black of the sky by Nalpur of Runn, the Merciful, the Beneficent."

"Tell us about it," Mirren asked.

Inibek Kob smiled and settled himself comfortably against the warm flank of Kel-Birat. "Long ago, shortly after the days of the beginning, on a certain night when Nalpur returned to his camp, he found that his cousin, Sasrank, had plundered his torka and driven his cattle away into the mountains. In furious pursuit he sprang from peak to peak across the mountains, but often he stumbled and fell into the canyons. He raged at the blackness of the sky that prevented him from seeing his way, so as he raced along he leaped up from the mountain peaks and stabbed the blackness with his sword."

Kob's two lieutenants and his men were nodding in agreement to the telling of the old story.

He continued: "There would be many more stars in the sky except that eventually Nalpur began to tire from his hurts when he fell into the canyons. Then his first companion, Karagh, took up the chase. But never could he catch Sasrank. Now the two small moons that follow each other closely across the sky, they are Sasrank and Karagh." Inibek pointed. The moons rose slowly from the horizon, shedding a soft pink light.

The fact that the two, with their pinkish reflections from the red sun, traveled at different rates of speed and sometimes were far apart, and sometimes one passed the other, did not affect the explanation. It was as it had always been, they just missed each other in the night. The ancient word took care of everything.

Everything but one.

Brian watched a large new star that had appeared not many nights ago—a star that traveled perceptibly among the other stars. This was not as things had always been.

Brian saw Inibek's worried face following the new star. "It was told us you are from the sky. Can you tell us of this new star?"

Brian was half expecting the question. "It is a star that brings much evil," he said.

"I feared it was an evil omen."

"But another star also approaches that brings much good. Only time will tell which accomplishes its purpose."

Rataq's eyes burned in the firelight. "It is only because there are two ships that there is evil. Just one would be good."

Brian thought of the Litanofoq zotoing Thana for slaves. He opened his mouth to speak, then he closed it again. This was neither the time nor the place.

There was a period of silence.

Then into the silence Inibek spoke casually. "Kors an Forstane, why do you seek Benjak?"

Just as casually Kors answered, "We invoke the old convenant of Nalpur of Runn. We seek refuge from our enemies."

"As blood brother, if indeed you are blood brother, you have the right. But these others. . . ."

"They are my companions. They helped us destroy the Vanth. Without them it would not have happened."

Inibek nodded. "I have heard something of that, and of a redbearded warrior—a messenger, it was said, from the Thana god Llu. This is he?"

"This is he."

Kob turned toward Brian. "Here we do not worship Llu, but we have respect for a warrior. And you bring along your women." Lit by the dying glow of the fire, Kob's face was grim as he looked at Kors. "I hope you truly are blood brother." Inibek kicked up the fire. "If the Vanth are destroyed, who then are your enemies?"

Brian answered. "Ones who come from the sky from the star with weapons that kill at a distance."

"You too come from the sky?"

Brian paused, seeking words that could make a grybin-riding nomad understand. "We come from a different sky," he said.

"The sky is not all the same?"

"The sky is very large. There are many different parts."

Kob place a bit of saad in his mouth, chewed thoughtfully. "If they command the sky and kill at distance, you are in danger wherever you run. You hide among the Kiyatagu, the Kiyatagu are in danger."

Kors looked Kob in the eye and spoke softly. "The covenant takes no heed of danger. It requires refuge."

Kob snapped, "We know the covenant. We know danger. We live with danger. But we do not invite it without reason." He gazed at Brian, and Mirren beside him, then turned his head to look at Rataq and Ngora. "I will talk with Benjak," he said, and leaned back against his grybin.

We are accepted for a few days, anyway, Brian thought.

Icy wind washed over the figures that huddled by the last coals of fire. Inibek Kob and his men now were dim leather-covered mounds, asleep as soon as they lay down. A single sentry paced slowly around the camp.

Ngora sat close beside Rataq, her patient. Beside the heat of the fire she had massaged his legs and back, kneading knotted muscles until, with the loosening and improved circulation, the soreness began to flow away. And again she oiled the skin of his face and the backs of his hands, as she had done before in the morning.

She explained, "The spectrum of this sun emits only a very limited fraction of its energy in the ultraviolet region. Still, at this altitude it can burn badly. We are acclimated, but you, even though your skin is pigmented as dark as mine, have never before been unprotected in the radiation of a sun. There is also the abrasive wind." Lightly she touched his cheek. "I can feel the inflammation beginning in the texture of your skin."

Rataq touched her hand. "You take good care of me."

She smiled. "I'm a doctor."

Rataq returned her smile, yawned, turned on his side and curled up, clutching his robe close about him.

Still awake and sitting up, Brian shivered and put his arm around Mirren, sat close for warmth. He felt the tension of her body as they both watched the new star. Dull red from the red sun, it progressed slowly and inexorably among the hard white stars, growing darker red in the twilight zone and finally blinking out into the night.

"What will they think when there are two red

stars? You told him, but he didn't understand. He puts it on a par with his Nalpur myth, and Nalpur of Runn will take care of it."

Brian carried on the thought. "When the shuttles land he will begin to wake up."

"We have to be sure they do land." Mirren's voice came out strained. "We have to find a way to communicate, to keep them away from Colufo. They are sure to pick up radiation from there. They will think we have something to do with it. They will time-stabilize an orbit above it and send in a shuttle."

"Let's relax, Mirren. This is a camping trip, a few days of R and R."

She shook her head. "You may call it rest and refreshment, but I'm sore from here to here." She laid one hand on the ground beside her, the other atop her head.

Brian grinned, "I'm a little stiff myself."

Already she was back to her fretting and she hardly heard him. "I'm worried. We have to use this time to do some planning."

"Planning, schmanning. We haven't the tools. All this is new. We have to learn the territory."

Mirren went on. "Perhaps we can have the tribe help us tramp out a great sign, one large enough to see from orbit. Make it say MAYDAY. That should bring a scouting shuttle down to us. Perhaps just LAND HERE would be better, not so disquieting."

"Aw, come off it. We have no idea what conditions we're heading into. It's dark as the night up there, with no stabbings from Nalpur of Runn to let in a speck of light. Somewhere along the way we will learn what we can do. Depend on it. Now take a vacation."

"I just can't think, I'm so tired and cold. I just can't think."

"Now you have put your finger on the right

button. Don't think. Some day we'll get you back to a control console once again. You can be boss. Right now, open up your cloak and we'll wrap both of them around us. Get some sleep." He pulled her close, kissed her, felt her relax in weariness.

Before Brian slept his mind went nibbling around a worry he had been keeping to himself. Rataq—was he really all that he said? The switch had been mighty fast, from leader of a landing party to running away with the only ones who might have made some sort of effective resistance. Still, it had to be fast or not at all. Was it just to get us away from control of the grounded ship at Colufo? Could they have planned the scene at landing, when Lazo Rataq made the switch? But how could it have been planned? And how could it have happened spontaneously, except in sincerity?

In the early morning, when hobbled grybins were gathered in, their frosty breath blew like smoke in the icy wind. After a breakfast of squares of waybread taken from saddle pouches, they moved out into the grassy sea that rolled to the edge of the great arc of the dark blue sky.

Brian had always been puzzled that such a red sun gave essentially a white light, but it did. The sky did seem a darker blue; maybe the greens were darker too. Clouds were red near the sun, a bright red. Then they faded as distance increased, taking on tints of red depending on the reflective angles and qualities of the particles of moisture. Perhaps if he could see the landscape in Earth sunlight the colors would be different, but with no comparison the light seened surprisingly similar.

After three hours of travel the sun burned hot and the wind blew hot. Robes were loosened. Ahead and far to the east, Brian saw dark specks moving. They disappeared in a fold of the land, then reappeared closer, moving swiftly. He wondered if that was good or bad, or nothing at all. Remembering that multifaceted eyes were not farsighted, he urged his mount up beside Inibek Kob.

"Would you expect friends or enemies?" He pointed.

Kob peered in the direction. "Unknowns are always enemies. But I see no one."

Kors moved up along with Brian. "His strange little eyes see far," he said.

Kob flicked his eyes from Kors back to Brian. "Even a stranger's warning should not be totally disregarded. How many?"

Brian gazed, attempting a count. "Many, a great many. Perhaps twenty times your troop here."

"Two hundred is an army," Kob said thoughtfully. "I would know if the Kiyatagu were riding. Are there no flocks, no tipulas with packs?"

"No flocks. No pack animals. Maybe some spare mounts."

"And riding fast?"

Brian nodded.

"They are enemy." He held up his hand for a halt.

"Are they coming straight toward us?"

"They will cross our path somewhat ahead."

"We wait here. I will go forward on foot with this Brian McCann to the rim. Come." He strode up the gentle rise.

Brian and Inibek crouched just below the top, while the rest waited among the small shrubs along the trickle of creek. The grybins browsed.

Brian lay tense, head just high enough to see over the grasses, watching the many figures disappear and then reappear, larger each time. He felt for the sword beside him and watched Kob, eyefolds straining wide, black fur on the back of his neck rising. How far did they have to come before he could see? At least the riders could see no farther than Inibek. Brian could make out details now—cloaked warriors, lances rising vertical, butts pocketed in long cylinders behind their saddle pads. A few long-legged high-altitude grybins in the lead, running, sailing in leaps over low shrubs. Brian wondered at the skill and balance of the riders and at the speed they were making. Why? Tribal warfare? How long could they keep up that pace?

Inibek slithered backward through the grass, pulled Brian back with him. "Sukota!" he whispered. "Many. Coming from the direction of our torkas, riding like the grass was afire behind them and a storm of wind was pushing it."

His face was grim. "I need to know why they ride here. Too many to fight," he muttered, as they hiked quietly down the slope.

Brian picked up the reins of his grybin to remount but Kob held his arm. He ordered Mirren, Ngora, Kors and Rataq to dismount. At his nod, five of his men, still mounted, each picked up the reins of one of the grybins.

Brian turned to face Inibek Kob chest to chest. He was a head taller. He looked down into the thousand tiny facets of his yellow eyes.

"Why do you put us afoot?"

The flash of Kob's hand came too fast to follow. Brian felt the knife edge touch his throat.

Kob's voice was calm. "There are too many to fight."

Brian lifted his hand to grasp Inibek's wrist. In his back he felt the pressure of a spear point. The lines of Kob's face hardened. Brian's grip rested only lightly on the wrist. All positions held. Brian felt his forehead wet with sweat, but his mouth was dry.

Kob continued, voice unchanged. "If they do not discover us, we go on as before. If they do, our grybins are fresher than theirs. Their remounts are too few to matter. If they discover us, we ride."

"And leave us!"

Kors spoke sharply. "This is not the refuge of the covenant."

Kob stared at him. "Dead, we will never be of help to you. Alive, perhaps we will, in time."

"But will we be alive?" Mirren asked.

Kob smiled. "A prize to be taken, strange outlanders to be examined. Pursuit is delayed." Abruptly he sheathed his knife and vaulted into his saddle.

They waited, still as the grass when no wind stirred.

An outrider from the Sukota trotted over the hilltop.

Inibek Kob picked up his single rein. "My friends, if Nalpur of Runn wills it, I shall see you again." He kneed Kel-Birat around. The Kiyatagu raced away.

"Some fighter," Brian said.

Kors answered. "If he is first companion to Benjak, he is a great fighter. If he is first companion to Benjak he is quick of mind; he measures odds. If he is first companion when the odds say run, he has the best grybin."

## five

The leather-robed Sukota pounded toward them through grass belly high on their horned grybins and humped-backed tipulas, lances and bows with arrows at the ready. The leader raced to within a couple of meters of the small group standing together and pulled up short, his grybin rearing against the pressure of the rein around its lower jaw, squalling with the suddenness and pain of it. The leader quickly waved half his army in pursuit of the fleeing Kiyatagu. Then he sat his still trembling mount, squat body proudly erect, staring at the five strangers through his slits of eye folds. He rotated his head in the typical tight circles, passing the image across multiple eye facets for better resolution, his mobile cat ears twisted forward.

Brian and Rataq both held right hands on their blasters.

Kors cautioned, "No use."

A hundred Sukota crowded around in a narrowing circle, dropping their folds down on their cheeks like outsized bags under their eyes. Hands reached out from the circle, pulled hoods back.

Out of her tension Mirren mocked, "Shall I drop the robe and model the latest in wornout one-piece uniforms for them?"

Kors said quickly, "Do that, all of you. The stranger you look the better."

Hands reached to finger hair and cloth. The leader jabbed his lance against Brian's chest.

"I am Xergin, deitch of Sukota. I am the garlon that stoops out of the sky with the swiftness of the wind to smash and hold my quarry with talons of steel. Who are you that rode with the Kiyatagu?"

Brian's mind raced, thinking of their confrontation yesterday with the Kiyatagu, when they had some reason to anticipate acceptance, perhaps friendship. Here there was no possible tie from the past. They were captured booty, only that.

He thrust his chest against the point of steel. "I come from another sun, another yann, down through the sky to see if there may be any brothers here with whom we may be friends. If so, perhaps we may learn things of value and from our knowledge teach something also."

Brian felt a jab after the word "teach." He gritted his teeth at the pain, but held his voice steady. "I can see by the way you ride like the cutting wind, and sit straight and tall like a tower of stone on your grand steed, that you are a great leader with a deep power over a strong clan in this land of grass and sky."

Brian watched his man relax and gaze around at his riders. "We would be friends to you." Brian went on, "But if combat is needful, I challenge you. You must be the greatest fighter of them all. I challenge you one on one." He let go of his blaster—they did not know yet that it was a weapon—and tugged his sword part way from its scabbard.

Xergin's dark face split and his white teeth gleamed in laughter. "For pleasure, for pleasure. But no time now. We just take you with us."

His eye caught the flashing color of the jewel Rataq wore. He clutched at it and jerked; the chain held. Rataq's head rocked like a child's bobbing toy.

Xergin released the jewel, set his lance in its leather cylinder, and whipped out his sword. "That jewel is mine and your head is in the way." He raised his sword.

Rataq closed his fist around his jewel, backed a step. A spear point dug into his back.

"Best give it to him," Brian said.

"I can't. I can't."

Xergin's sword poised at the top of his backswing.

Kors spoke quickly. "A stranger's life is of no value; he is not bluffing."

Brian held his voice calm. "No matter how important that jewel is, it cannot be more important than your head."

Slowly, deliberately, his eyes fixed steadily on Xergin, Rataq unclasped the chain, but his hands were shaking. His voice came out strained and highpitched. "Beware; the power of this jewel will destroy any but the rightful owner."

Brian had not seen Rataq at any time before so clearly distressed.

Xergin laughed again. "I am the one whose threats have meaning." He gazed with nutating head at the jewel in his hand, then slipped the chain over his head.

He thrust his mount past Brian, Rataq and Kors to look more closely at Mirren and Ngora. In passing he said, "You are Thana. You did not come from the sky. Do you guide these sky people to our land?"

Kors nodded. "I do."

Xergin grunted. He poked with his sword at Mirren's shoulder, forcing her to turn around while he looked her over. Brian tugged at his sword, but a spear cracked down on his wrist. He looked up into the tough black furry face of a tribesman.

Xergin pricked Ngora around in the same way, then made a noise in his throat and spoke. "Your women are very different—big and black, lean and white. They will be interesting." He turned to his closest men.

"Take weapons. Give them grybins."

They took the swords from Brian and Kors and took Kors' bow and arrows, but they did not take the blasters from Brian and Rataq. Brian felt a jump of hope.

As soon as he had the chance, Brian whispered to Rataq, "What was the jewel?"

Rataq hesitated, then answered, "My communicator. I am cut off from my people."

Brian could understand the downcast feeling. Communication was his desperate need too, but a question stirred in his mind. Why had Rataq not disclosed before that he had such means of communication?

As they began to ride, Brian became aware of another prisoner, the only woman with the Sukota. Who was she, the one woman with all these men? He watched her ride, sitting her mount tall as any man here, face grim, defiant. No surrender in her, Brian thought; she's tough as hammered steel.

All day they rode hard across a green land under an empty sky, always driving into a cutting wind. It had been biting cold at night and now blew parching hot, with the red sun burning high. After many months on Vassa, Brian still had an uneasy feeling about that sun. A sun should not be so large, so close and so red. At night they had worn their cloaks close around them against the cold and the freezing wind. Now they wore them loose against the heat and the dehydrating blasts.

On the third day he noticed that the grass was no

longer lush and green. Now it grew in scattered tufts, the spring growth already drying. The water in the pool where they finally halted, late in the evening, tasted saltish and foul.

At first light next day the Sukota prodded them awake. A few minutes to eat the last scraps of waybread and to fill their bottles with brackish water, and they were on their way again.

This day the land became true desert, with the red sun rising in a hot yellow sky. The only vegetation was widely scattered bushes armed with long curved thorns, and rare white-topped tufts of grass. Even these were barbed. From trotting grybins' feet rose puffs of white acrid dust that burned in the nostrils. Sweat soaked the dust into mud on necks, foreheads and eye corners, then dried, leaving tingly stinging cakes that felt as if they too were barbed.

This day the Sukota needed meat. They did not ride in a compact body as before, but spread wide for hunting along the way. Even here there was game, if one had eyes to find it.

Rataq's riding ability had improved rapidly since his first day on a grybin. On level ground the past three days, he had not fallen. But today the strain of hard riding showed. The roundness of his face was gone, his eyes were bloodshot, the strength to grip with his legs was failing, his sense of balance was erratic.

Brian stayed close to keep an eye on him as gradually they fell farther and farther behind the group. Only the two specifically asigned to guard stayed near.

Brian was ready when Rataq finally lost control, slid off his mount and rolled in the sand. Jerking his grybin to a halt, Brian hopped off to help. But before he took two steps he saw his guard bearing down on him, heels kicking his grybin's ribs. His yellow eyes gleamed. His body leaned forward, clutching his lance with hand and arm, the tip lowered to strike. The guard's mouth was open, yelling.

Brian heard no words, just a drawn out, "Ah... ah yi."

No time to think, only to react. He dove, rolling into the grybin's feet. A tangle of Brian and legs and hooves and the lance. Brian felt a hoof stamp his thigh. The grybin tumbled; the lance point stuck in the ground. The man vaulted upward and flew wildly over the grybin's head, arms flailing. He landed heavily and lay still.

Brian came up limping and looked for Rataq. He still lay in the sand, with the mounted Sukota pricking at his back with his lance point. Just then Rataq rolled over and blew him off his grybin with his blaster.

Rataq gritted through dried-out cracking lips, "There is still no one here to know this is a weapon." He thrust it back into its holster as Brian helped him to his feet. They watched the backs of the Sukota disappearing over the brow of a hill with Mirren, Ngora and Kors among them. No one turned, no one noticed. The last sight Brian remembered was Mirren, tall, graceful, swaying to the pacing stride of her mount in silhouette against the skyline.

"Quarks to parsecs!" Brian gazed around at the bleak desolation of sand and rock. "Being free from the Sukota is no great thing." He brushed sticking sand from the side of his face. "And I would not have picked this dry-as-dust inferno. The devil himself would be at home here."

He limped after his grybin and led it back toward Rataq. Except for the one that lay as still as its rider, the grybins had bolted. He untied the water bottle from the saddle pad of that one and tossed it to Rataq.

"They know where the next water is. We had best mount up and be after them."

Rataq stared, his dark eyes opened wide. "After them! Be captured again and lose all I have gained?"

Brian felt the rush of blood, the rise of pressure in his brain, his pulse pounding in his ears. "You acted with intent, in this desert? You idiot!"

Rataq looked shocked, tugged at his blaster. "No man calls me idiot."

"I call you idiot."

They glared at each other, each with a blaster in his grip. Gradually Brian pinched off his anger. "We are both idiots. We do not make peace between our races this way." He rammed his blaster back into its holster. "But why did you do it here?"

Rataq grinned. "I could not endure riding on that jarring animal any longer. I selected a time when we had opportunity. You come through very nicely."

Brian grunted. "We can still catch them." He bellied across the grybin, swung around to sit and reached out a hand to Rataq.

"No. I go this way." Rataq started on foot along the hill. "Come quickly. They will be back looking for us."

"There is no water. We have no guide. We will fry in the sun."

Lazo Rataq plodded on with no pause.

Brian sat on his grybin muttering, "Double idiot." Oh, Brian Boru, my ancient ancestor, what do I do now? I know what you would say: "The mission comes first. Slender as it is, Rataq is the only thread that leads toward a possibility of peaceful settlement of Vassa. The mission comes first. You can always find another woman." He sighed. "You are a cad, Brian Boru." He urged the grybin along after Rataq while he thought about Mirren and Ngora. He shrugged. They each had a blaster under their robes; they were not totally defenseless.

He caught up with Rataq and helped him up behind to ride double.

The land before them was harsh and dry as bare bones stripped by vultures, polished by the wind and baked by the sun. Behind them the blowing wind began to drift sand into their tracks. Soon there would be nothing but the wind's own private patterns.

Sometimes riding, sometimes walking, they struggled up and down across a series of rolling dunes, cursing the loose sand until they came to a stretch where the wind had blown all the sand away, leaving only a shingle of fist-sized gravel that cut the feet and hands and knees when they stumbled. Then they wished for sand again.

Except for the susurrous rush of air past their ears they were wrapped in the silence of the desert and the heat of the scorching sun. Brian felt sweat rolling down his ribs under his arms and thought to throw off his robe, but he knew that meant he would dehydrate faster. He shook his water bottle.

"Not much left."

Rataq turned his up. "Empty. Let us go find some more." Brian waved his hand toward the mountains he saw low and dark in the distance. "To be sure, there may be water somewhere within a hundred kilometers, but I do not know where."

"Maybe you had better call and find out, or get help, or something."

"Call? With what?"

"You have the technology. Surely you would not travel without some means of communication."

Brian felt the pressure of anger rising again. How could this idiot understand so little? He clamped control on his voice. "You forget, when your Rogo forced our ships to crash we lost our technology and nearly all our people."

Rataq nodded, his voice matter of fact. "We can't help that now." He stopped suddenly. "You mean there is no communication? We are alone with no help?"

"Exactly."

Rataq was slow in answering. "Had I known, I would have fought for my micheli." His hand reached up to his chest for the jewel that was no longer there. "I thought you were concealing . . . but to have nothing. . . ."

"This world is larger than a space ship."

Rataq's eyes were worried. "Where do we go now?"

Brian pointed. "We go toward the peaks of those dark mountains on the horizon and pray we find, in time, a trickle coming down a valley."

Loose sand breaking like white surf against bare rock, hard-baked alkali flats rosy pink, reflecting the sun, brutal shingle, then a long slope of lava, frozen froth of black mineral surf. They shambled and staggered over one after the other, alternately riding and walking.

Brian's worn shoes were disintegrating step by step. He envied Rataq's soft boots, designed for smooth metal corridors but holding up among the rocks, and his silvery unisuit, shedding dirt, sand and stain and still gleaming under the loose flapping leather cloak.

The soft pads behind the grybins' horny hooves were pierced and torn.

The three limped grimly on. Waves of heat quivered up from heated rock. Ahead, the mountains seemed to rise and float on a tremulous lake.

"I see water," Rataq burst out excited.

"Mirage," Brian said flatly.

"I know water." He began to run.

Brian rode calmly after him. He thought, he has much to learn about living on a planet. When Rataq fell, exhausted, Brian hoisted him onto the grybin. Walking beside, he held him there until Rataq could sit by himself.

As the sun dropped lower the mirage faded. Brian raised his eyes to the mountains. They seemed no nearer, in spite of the hours of dogged travel. High in the mountains he saw a sparkle of light—red light, a pinpoint only. A fire? It must be larger than a campfire, to be visible at this distance, and the pinpoint was so bright it hurt his eyes. What else? Without thinking—he was beyond organized thinking—because it was a specific goal rather than an extended line of heights, he headed toward it.

They floundered on, consciousness fading except for the dull aching drive to keep moving. As twilight darkened the light winked out. Fuzzy headed, Brian wondered, did they put out a fire at night?

They plodded onward in the coolness until the wind turned icy. Then they hobbled the grybin and sheltered in the lee of a rock, drawing their cloaks close about them.

In the early morning Brian found the grybin close by, standing with neck lowered, ears drooping, eyes hooded. He heaved a great sigh as Brian saddled up, and after they climbed on, he slouched a few steps and stopped.

"What do we do now?"

Brian growled, "Show him who's boss." He kicked hard with his heels. They both kicked hard with their heels. For a result they obtained only a grunt. Brian got off to get a stick.

"The animal is boss." Rataq grinned through cracked lips.

Brian looked at the grybin. It was haggard and wasted, flesh dissolved away, bones thrusting out of the skin. Brian threw away the stick and they both walked, leading the grybin.

In late morning heat, through the dull grayness that muffled all his senses, Brian saw the grybin's ears prick forward, his nostrils open wide, sniffing. Rataq croaked, "He is interested in something?"

"Water, maybe."

They mounted, letting the rein hang free. The grybin moved, lifting its pace to a shaky trot toward a rocky outcropping.

Between them and the rocks they saw a scattering of white objects. Closer, they saw that they were bones, bleached white in the sun: a skull with horns, a grybin once, and the skulls of other animals.

Brian shook his head to clear his bedazzled eyes. He picked up the rein, hauled it back. There were too many bones scattered haphazardly. Hard mouthed, the grybin drove onward.

"He really does smell water?" Rataq asked.

"Something's wrong."

The grybin fought, lowered head pulled down and back, snapping his head from side to side, jerking Brian's hands back and forth. Brian eased off. He did not want to dump all of them on the ground.

But why so many bones here? They had seen none before. Every nerve in his body hammered. Then he saw, he knew. There was water, and it was guarded.

## six

Small four-legged bodies rushed toward them past desert thorn bushes, great heads bobbing—a troop of doglike animals. Their enormous heads, seeming too big for their bodies, were all red slavering mouths and great gaping jaws with row on row of needle-pointed teeth.

"Stril!" Brian yelled. He pulled his blaster. The grybin snorted in fear, and Brian felt a tremor travel through its body. It reared. Rataq began to slip.

"Hang on!" Brian shouted. "The bite is poison. Death."

The grybin wheeled, terror stricken, to rush away. For a short distance it pulled ahead. Then it floundered to a halt. Exhausted, it stood shivering, eyes rolling in panic.

"Use your gun. You will never need it more. Take the right side; I'll take the left."

The great open mouths on four short legs dashed in randomly. Brian and Rataq tried to shoot each one. For the charge to last, they thumbed down the controls for a needle ray that sliced flesh like a cauterizing knife. Parts of bodies carved off with no bleeding.

There were too many, charging too fast. Nips

above the grybin's heels. One leaped up to clamp its jaws on the hamstring. Rataq's ray severed the head, but still it clung.

Harrowing shudders convulsed the grybin's body. It sank to its knees, toppled over. Brian and Rataq jumped off, stood back to back firing at any stril that left the mass circling about them.

But now half the pack were dead, cut into quivering pieces.

"How is your charge?"

"Beginning to weaken."

"Can't just stand here. They're keeping their distance. Move toward the outcrop, the spring must be there below it."

Back to back, step by step, warily they eased their way.

One of the stril, circling, all its attention on Brian, dashed into a clump of bushes, all white branches and long thorns. It yelped in pain, struggled to get away. Cruel dead-white thorns curved and clung. The bush moved, Brian saw it creep to surround the frantic animal. Yelps became screams as the bush contracted and more and more of the thorns pierced. Finally screams and struggles ceased. The stril, almost completely hidden by the branches, lay still.

"Remind me to stay clear of thorn bushes," Brian muttered.

"Stril!" Rataq yelled.

Brian jerked his eyes away. Rataq's shot sliced the jumping stril. It dropped at Brian's feet. He crouched, ready for more, but the rest broke away, all racing to be first at the feast on the grybin. Brian and Rataq descended to the pool in a basin below the rock.

"That's one I owe you," Brian said.

After drinking and filling their bottles, they started again toward the mountains. While the stril were gorging on the grybin, and their own dead also, the two of them must go far enough into the desert so there would be no pursuit. It was clear that the stril waited near the water for their meals to come to them.

They had a bottle of water each, no food, no prospects, no grybin; tattered shoes, cut feet bleeding, Rataq's wonderful soft shoes intact but his feet inside bruised and beaten. He limped as badly as Brian did.

Grasp the mind, point it at the hills. Do not let it think on hurt. Step after step uncounted, unfelt, lugging through sand, stumbling over shingle, eyes aching from glare, they continued hot staggering kilometers, brains baking in the ovens of their skulls.

That was when the hallucinations started. Rataq heard Eckem Meluq calling him. Then he saw him, stuffed as always into his command chair not twenty paces away on a black desert rock. He wore an obese grin on his mottled face.

"Make ready; Ubeq and Barsorq are coming for you."

Rataq stopped in his tracks. "You swork!" he yelled. "You fat swork!" He laughed. "I never called you that before to your face. How do you like it now?" His laugh became hysterical, his eyes unfocused. "You swork, I'm going to jam your head down into your shoulders. It will be easy, you're soft all over." He started off toward the rock, stumbled, fell on his face.

Brian helped him up, started him again toward the hills. Rataq jerked away. "Eckem Meluq can't stop me. Barsorq can't stop me. You can't stop me." He brushed his hand across his eyes. "Who are you, anyway?"

Brian took his elbow again, kept him moving in the right direction.

Rataq shook him off. "This is my world. I will conquer it."

"Our world," Brian said. "And the Thanas' world."

Rataq strained to focus on Brian. "Okay, our world, but the Thana are our drudges." He tried to smile with his cracked lips. "I'll give you this part of it."

Brian let the part about Thana pass, but it was something to remember.

Their trail was wobbling back and forth, but always heading toward the mountains.

"All those micros about the old Vassa did not show me this," Rataq mumbled. His voice sounded without timber, childish. "Bird songs. I do not hear any bird songs." His eyes were glazed again. "The micros told of green valleys, winding rivers, birds. This cannot be Vassa. We have landed on the wrong planet. You have deceived me!" He tugged awkardly at his blaster.

Brian spoke calmly. "Take a sip of your water if you have any left."

"Yes, water. Water." He stopped trying to pull his blaster, fumbled out the stopper of his leather bottle, held it to his lips, barely enough to wet his tongue. He licked inside the rim for the last moisture. "Will there be water there?" He waved ahead with his empty bottle.

"There will be water." Brian took one mouthful from his own bottle, ran the tepid leather-tasting wet around his mouth and swallowed. One mouthful left. "But we must find it."

When he drank, Brian lifted his eyes to the hills. Slowly it entered his stultified brain that he saw something—that red light again. It was closer now, much larger, fiercely bright high up on the mountain, and too steady to be a fire.

Before them another salt pan. Flat, easy going.

Legs continued moving while the sun settled slowly and the heat drained away out of the air. Then abruptly the flat ceased, cut away at the edge of a cliff. They gazed down into a great depression lying across their way to the mountains. In the depths they could see traces of a winding river bed, but they saw no water. Brian groaned; another obstacle.

There was no time to find a way down before dark, but they did find a ledge below the rim that sheltered them somewhat from the wind. Backs against the rock, they sat side by side, wrapped in their robes.

Rataq's shaky voice came scarcely above a whisper. "Are we going to live through this?"

"We can't plan on anything else." Plans, Brian thought, plans to save a war, but can't plan a day.

"And I guess. . . ."

Brian felt Rataq struggling for words. When he had landed on Vassa he was ready with words, full of them, glib. Now he stuttered.

"I guess I should . . . I should thank you for saving . . . I could not have made it alone."

Brian caught on. Pride had great difficulty admitting it was not equal to any problem whatsoever. But then a certain pride is needed for a man to hold his head up and look the world in the eye. And Rataq had guts, too. After his soft living in the low gravity of the ship, he had guts to last this long.

"I could not make it alone either," Brian said.

They sat silent in the dark together. Brian stared out from the ledge. This time there were stars in the black. The last time he sat in darkness on a ledge, in a deep cave, there were no stars; there were visions. This time he had less confidence in living through the next day. If there is water in the valley . . . . And Mirren. He remembered the feeling of his arms around her. Would he ever find her again?

In the night Brian felt Rataq shivering and mumbling to himself. Some of the words came clear. "If I ever see that Inibek Kob again, I will have his bones broken one by one."

Brian grinned in the darkness. "Hold your rage close. Maybe it will keep you warm."

"Swork!" was the only answer.

"For myself," Brian went on, "I'd like to see him right now, with spare grybins and a full water bottle."

"Well, in that case, I will not have his bones broken until later." He pulled his robe tighter around his body. "If what is hard won is of greater value, I am going to place high worth on this land."

"You said I could have this part." Brian's laugh was a hoarse bark.

Half a day to climb zigzag down the cliff. Then they shambled on weak and trembly legs toward the dry river bed.

Rataq's voice was a rasping whisper. "I can walk if I can stay on my feet. Do not let me fall." His eyes stared down at the ground, watching every step.

Brian felt a breath of cold air, but the hot red sun still burned high. He raised his head to look toward the mountains. There was a cloud, a towering cumulonimbus rolling mass of cloud piled on mass, gray and darker gray below. At the ground, black.

Rain? They stood watching. The tongue of cold air flowed down the foothills toward them, dropped down the cliff opposite, spread and crossed the floor of the valley. With a cold ferocity the turbulent churning air enveloped them. The black cloud roared. Dust, sand, bits of debris, salt stung faces and eyes, but no rain.

Rataq grabbed Brian's arm to keep from being blown away. They both dropped to the ground.

"Where's rain?" yelled Rataq, scarcely making a sound.

But the rain was still far away on the hills.

They lay still, faces against the ground. They could have relaxed there forever, but the drive to move toward the hope of water was still strong. Blindly they crawled, staying together by touch.

Suddenly there were figures in the flying dust, dim shades walking, leading grybins, silent figures, all sound lost in the roar of the wind. Figures muffled to the eyes in the robes of Thana-Kovas, with dust veils covering their faces. Wraiths appearing, disappearing, visible for a moment only and gone.

A foot brushed against Brian's shoulder. A man stooped to look into his face. Brian could not see beyond the coarse threads of the veil. A second Kovas, leading another grybin, stopped. Brian felt himself lifted, tossed across a saddle pad, head and arms hanging, legs on the other side. A hand held him at the knee.

Rataq. He could only assume they carried him also. They had been together, touching. They could not find one without the other, could they? Head hanging down, he lost consciousness.

He was conscious again, or was he dreaming? He heard water, the continuing splatter of falling water, smelled water, felt the dampness of moist air against his cheek. He was dreaming. He held his eyelids closed to save the feel, the memory of water. The sound continued, the feel of dampness. Cautiously he opened an eye. There was falling water, a thin white ruffled column plunging from high on the dark cliff, splashing on a jagged pile of black gneiss at the edge of a cool pool. The arc of a rainbow quivered mistily in the spray.

Brian sat up. The sun shone low, the heat of the day gone, the cold of the night not yet come. He sat on the flat top of a huge tawny rounded stone. Beside him, Rataq was beginning to stir. From behind a voice spoke.

"They are coming to."

Thana-Kovas gave them water and waybread. Brian drank a few swallows, ate a few mouthfuls. He wanted more, but it did not go down easily. And who were these tribesmen?

He faced around. A small stream gurgled from the pool through a grove of broad-leafed trees. Throughout the grove there were Kovas, sitting eating or lying resting. Everyone held the rein of a grybin and a remount.

A large man stalked toward him, heavily muscled, square faced. Brian looked into the bulging yellow eyes in the black furred face. He recognized Inibek Kob.

Trying to stand to meet him, Brian staggered, feeling for his balance with benumbed feet and legs. Kob stood, large hands on hips, before him. There was tension in his face. He held his body taut like a steel spring locked by a cam that was ready to pop. His words snapped.

"Can you ride?"

"Yes." Brian looked down at Rataq.

He nodded, struggling to his feet.

Kob turned, waved and shouted to his men. He waited for them to bring grybins for Brian and Rataq. When he turned back his face relaxed to deep sorrow.

"You were my guests, and I abandoned you; you would have sat on a stool beside the fire in my tent and dipped four fingers into my meat bowl, yet I abandoned you. Still, it was a thing that was needful. When a wagon wheel breaks the wagon cannot move. But you have escaped and have taken no great hurt? And the others, they are still with the Sukota?"

"Yes, that is true."

His face twisted, grim. "We will see them again. While I was away the Sukota swept down on our camp. My first companion, Benjak, deitch of the Kiyatagu, is gored in the leg with a poisoned spear. He lives but he cannot ride. Our flocks are scattered. Oveda, our wife, is stolen. Our churns are broken; the fires in our tents are stamped out. I have gathered some of our clan. We ride."

"The Sukota?"

"The Sukota. They rode far around to make us believe they were Juro or Buka, but we saw them. You saw them. They were Sukota. This way by the valley is shorter. We will arrive before they can believe." He drew his sword, slashed the air.

"It is not friendly to steal women, but we all do it on occasion. And afterward we do not make a great fuss. Still, Oveda is more than most. The insult is more than we can bear."

Looking at Inibek's troubled face and averted eyes, Brian thought, he cares a great deal about this woman, but in his culture one does not admit it.

They rode.

## seven

Eckem Meluq saw the red signal light #87 beside the comm screen blinking. That was Barsorq's number on the surface of Vassa. "About time he called in," Meluq grumbled, and punched the button beside the light.

Barsorq sat at the console of the grounded ship at Colufo. The deep creases of his rumpled face sagged. His eyes were bloodshot with fatigue.

"Report," barked Eckem Meluq.

"Yes, Eckem, swar." He bowed his head slightly and touched his fingers to his chin in the Litanofoq salute. "I am pleased to report that survey and requisition are going well. Many stores of foodstuffs, bread grains and other nutritious seeds, edible tubers, cheeses and so on have been located and donated." A smile fluttered for a moment on his thin lips. "These supplies are now in the process of being transported to certain suitable houses in Colufo that have been released to us for storage."

"Fine, fine," Meluq said rapidly. "But what news have you of Rataq?"

"Well, swar, Ubeq has zotoized numerous Thana and. . . ."

Eckem Meluq interrupted, "Don't tell me about

Ubeq! Tell me about Rataq."

"We have learned that he has fled with the three Earthians to the high plateau many obus east. Also we have learned who is their Thana guide, one named Kors Forstane an Tsankta. Zoto control has been implanted in the co-husband of this Thana, a man named Cogbard Rulerga an Tsankta. He has been flown beyond the canyon entrance to that plateau. When he finds them we will know."

"Swork, by smarsh! You haven't found him yet!" Meluq glared at the comm screen. "He was plotting against me. Me! Others are in the plot too. I want Rataq—alive, at least at first." He leaned back in satisfaction at the thought.

"What was this co-husband thing you said?"

"That is the way their families are. They believe two husbands are necessary to beget."

Meluq paused, considering. "Very fanciful." Then his voice snapped like a rawhide whip. "Now get him!" He broke connection.

Inibek Kob's scouts located the Sukota camp in a narrow riverine valley. During the night the Kiyatagu moved close, readying for the final rush. Inibek and Brian crept through the high grass to look over the brow into the valley campsite.

"Tell me what you see," whispered Inibek.

"Too dark for me. Can you see in the dark? Kors can see."

"Thana of the coast, who once were the cave-dwelling Thana, they see in the dark, but we do not."

In silence they peered down into the camp. Behind them were faint rustlings, a whispered word, the soft blowing of a grybin's breath through nostrils held nearly closed by Thana fingers to stop any call of grybin to grybin as they formed up.

Fifty Kiyatagu poised beside fifty mounts, holding themselves alert, waiting. Brian felt pressure building inside him. Consciously he slowed his breathing, felt the indrawn icy air all the way down into his lungs, shivered under his leather cloak.

As first dawn light began to gray the valley, he heard muffled noise coming from the camp, the first few women starting morning fires. Brian thought about their number: only fifty. And there had been at least two hundred in the Sukota raid. On their home ground there would be more. In a flash of memory he saw himself aching for action, any kind of action, during the months at Colufo in the dragging wait for the Litani to arrive. Now he was trapped into action that was no part of his choice. His fist clamped tight around the roughened grip of his sword hilt. The hard knot in his stomach drew tighter, like wet rawhide drying in the hot sun. But fifty crashing down into camp with surprise on unsuspecting, unready, half awakened. . . . It might do.

Kob and Brian slipped back from the edge to their mounts. Kob whispered, "When I see the smoke rise from their tents, I signal."

The whisper passed on. Little by little they began to see each other, a denser darkness against the dark. There was the light rattling of arrows being loosened in quivers, the soft scrape of lances being drawn from holders.

Kob, with Brian still beside him, mounted and walked his grybin slowly forward to the rim of the hill.

Now Brian could see the tops of the rounded tent huts, gray-white mounds crouching among trees and brush beside the river.

Inibek raised his arm and held it aloft for

everyone to see it against the sky. Now Brian could make out thin gray wisps of smoke coming from the black holes in the center of the gray-white mounds. Inibek swept down his arm with a large motion. His men started, and thundered down off the grassy hill. Their savage yells, bloodlusting, whipped through the sleeping camp. Weapons held high in murderous fists, they raged under the trees, through gaps in the brush, to the squatting tent huts, past the tents and the wagons drawn up beside them, past everything to the bank of the river.

They had expected screaming women and children scattering in panic. They had expected men—warriors—leaping for weapons, darting out from the flaps of their doorways. Instead there was only stillness: no movement save their own slashing ride; no sound save their own savage shouts. The rounded tent huts crouched silent, door flaps hanging with no motion.

The hilt of his sword was wet, slippery with his own sweat. Brian gripped it tighter. Had they been warned?

At the river they wheeled their grybins and started back, slowing to a walk. They dropped their dust veils to peer into bushes, around trees. Where were the Sukota?

Then burst the storm of arrows. Then flew the volley of spears. Then screamed the earpiercing yells of attacking Sukota, rising from cover in the bushes, rising from wagons, darting from behind rocks and trees.

After the point-blank hail of missiles, Sukota warriors leaped three and four to one, swarming over the reeling Kiyatagu. They fell, nocking arrows to bowstrings. They fell drawing swords from scabbards; they fell charging with lances.

Brian rushed a group, sword swinging, leaning

to his right to cut down a man. A Sukota on his left, grasping his ankle, thrust upward. Brian fell sprawling on top of the man he had just cut down. Before he could recover, Sukota were on him, lashing his hands together behind his back.

Inibek Kob cast his lance like a light javelin at the nearest Sukota. Then he drove Kel-Birat into the thick of the melee, whirling his great ax. He made great slaughter, and Kel-Birat reared to fight with his forefeet, then lashed out behind with his rear. Still the Sukota were too many. Finally the grybin could no longer keep his footing among the bodies. He stumbled and fell, casting Inibek head first against a tree.

Brian's neck ached from the thick wooden puno collar that kept his chin stretched always upward and the skin on his shoulders rubbed raw. It was even difficult to open his mouth enough to eat the logget gruel, nearly impossible to chew the tough meat scraps. His wrists were anchored at the extended corners of the diamond-shaped collar, one at the wrought-iron hinge and the other by the heavy lock opposite. Iron edges dug in. It felt like being in the stocks of ancient times, except that he carried the pillory around with him and slept—or tried to sleep—in it.

Curious Sukota women pulled his hair, pinched his skin, poked at his eyes, while their men laughed at his misery. And always a young Sukota held the end of a rawhide tether attached to the collar, ready to call a warning. But even if he escaped from his watcher, there was noplace to go. Along the river the Sukoya were thick. On the steppe they could easily run him down.

His thoughts rubbed his mind as raw as the galling collar on his shoulders. He had not yet found Mirren. He was no closer to preparing for the

*Plymouth*'s safe landing than he had been while dying of thirst on the desert. This was an unknown he had not thought of.

On the second day, McCann, Rataq, Kob and his two remaining tribesmen were summoned to Xergin's torka. An adult Sukota called Ogum hauled Brian along by his tether. When Brian set his heels to hold back, a jerk instructed about authority and obedience. He stumbled to his knees. The stocky Sukota laughed and kept jerking the line. The group gathered before the deitch's torka laughed. Brian scrambled forward, struggling to rise to his feet. Bitter hot blood raged through his veins. With stumbling steps he flung himself at the legs of the Sukota. They toppled to the ground together, but Brian staggered to his feet while the Sukota, still on his knees, scrabbled for the end of the tether. Just as he grasped it, Brian jerked it away. He pursued on his knees. The other Sukota began to laugh. When finally he laid hold of it, Brian jerked again, with his whole body in the movement. It cost him a hard gouge at the back of his neck, but the Sukota sprawled on his face. Now the other Sukota roared. Brian grinned through the pain of his neck and bloody shoulders, and stalked untethered through the open door of Xergin's torka, where Inibek had already entered. Kors was there too, also with a puno collar.

Brian halted before a small fire in the center. "Mirren, Ngora?" He mouthed the words toward Kors.

"Another part of the camp," he answered, and received a jerk at his collar.

A thin gray column of smoke rose up toward the opening in the tent roof. In the half light across the fire Brian could see a great wooden bed frame piled with furs where sat Xergin and Togrel. One each side of the frame, along the tent wall, were chests piled on chests, and over them he could see the upper part of the folding wooden lattice that held up the matted hair sides of the torka. Behind the men hung a leather decoration with colored designs. Everywhere overlapping tanned hides completely covered the ground, except for the fire circle. And everywhere crowding around were curious Sukota faces, bug eyes reflecting thousands of pinpoints of firelight.

Beside Xergin and Togrel, first companions, co-husbands, stood their wife, Ulfilas, her hand on Xergin's shoulder. She wore the typical leather cloak, secured at the shoulder by a fist-sized brooch embellished by a great green stone.

Rataq gasped but kept his voice low and spoke in Earth. "My jewel! They have separated it, destroyed it. I am alone, cut off. There will be no way to make contact. There is no longer hope."

Wearing only the Thana harness with sheathed knives, the men revealed similar short stocky bodies, but Xergin was a bit wider and thicker. Light-brown fur on their chests shaded to darker brown around their sides. The two sat with backs straight, unsupported, feet set solid on the ground cover, knees far apart—bowed by growing up on grybinback, where the knees were always far apart—black furred hands on black furred knees, arms straight from the shoulder: rigid poses, stern faces of judges holding court.

Brian's neck was a column of pain. Blood from the torn skin of his shoulders seeped through the shirt of his ragged uniform. He heard someone describing the incident outside.

". . . in his shame he ran away."

Brian watched Xergin's face closely; black lips grim, face set in the expression of one whose word is obeyed. With no change in his expression he said, "Ogum was not equal to his task. A man not equal to his charge is worth not even a worn magli hide." He shrugged. "Bring in the one."

Xergin pulled his shoulders back, folded his arms across his chest. "Inibek Kob, first companion of Benjak, deitch of the Kiyatagu, I have had you brought so that you would know."

What does this mean? wondered Brian.

A Thana-Kovas was led in and around behind everyone until he faced the fire between Inibek and Xergin. Lean and dark, a knife of a man, brown darker than most, eye color more orange than yellow. His eyes shifted rapidly from Xergin and Togrel to Kob and back, his lips drawn back in a satisfied smirk.

Kob tensed and muttered, "What is this?"

Xergin spoke. "You know this man?"

"I know him. He was my slave, the one who stood by my tent flap to admit or not to admit, at my order. Yes, I know him. I thought he was lost in the sandstorm."

Xergin relaxed. "He has done us a great favor. He brought us warning so that we were ready when you appeared." He exchanged glances with Togrel beside him. "Was that not a good deed to be rewarded?"

Kob spat into the fire. "Betrayed by a trusted man. A good deed for you, aye, a good deed. I would know how to reward it."

"And how would that be?"

"I would separate that head from its shoulders. I would not do it swiftly with one blow. I would do it gently so that it would take many chops to finish."

The slave's smirk died. He shrank back away from Inibek. The smell of fear filled the air around him. He turned to Xergin, pleading. Words tumbled one upon the other. "You said I brought you news that saved you, your people, yourself. I rode hard, I rode through dust and sand, I rode without stopping for sleep or food or water. I rode until the grybin under me could run no more and dropped to his knees and fell over dead in the grass. Then I ran, I ran until I brought you the news that saved you."

"So you did, so you did." Xergin turned to Togrel. "How should we reward him?"

Togrel spoke slowly, solemnly, a pronouncement. "One who is not loyal to his master can be loyal to no one. There is no pardon for a man who has raised his hand against his lord. But a reward we will give you. Let his head be struck off swiftly, not with many chops, but cleanly with one blow only."

## eight

A few more days only they remained in the shade by the cool running river before Xergin and Togrel declared a move. Tribes with large herds must change locations often for clean ground and untrampled grass.

In the cool of the early morning and evening they pushed their various flocks over the steppe toward the next water. In the heat of the day they rested. The animals were separated into droves. The koano plodded in front, ponderous, slow witted, with Sukota riding along the sides and behind, prodding them onward. The Koano depended for safety not on speed but on armor, a thick green hide plus horns, a pair just above the nostrils. A slow beast, but quick and clever with those sharp horns, hooking upward from close to the ground. The koano cows, mesors, provided milk. The tough koano hides made shields and saddles. The thinner softer skin of their bellies made the leather cloaks, one hide being enough for one cloak.

Behind the koano roamed the gayhearted magli, forever breaking out of formation and being driven back again, a shaggy animal able to feed on short grass the koano passed by. They too provided milk and the best-tasting meat, and their long hair, beaten together, pressed and matted, made the coverings for the torkas.

Out to one side were herded the spare grybins, and finally came the pack animals—long-necked tipula, not fast but long enduring with heavy loads; then the wide-bodied, donkeylike guams pulling carts, and the oxen of the koana dragging high-wheeled wagons. On these the matted hair coverings for the tent huts were rolled and tied, and the latticewood torka frames, the beds, the baskets, the cooking pots and tripods, the leather sacks for kukri, the rinn churns, the anvils and hammers, the skins for leather and for furs, all piled on the wagons and the carts and on the tipula, all secured with braided ropes. Everything a man needed for living on the steppe moved with him—his flocks, his grybins, his weapons, his shelter, his women and his tribesmen.

A host of men and animals and vehicles trekked across the prairie. A dust cloud pounded behind them. On the comm screen of the orbiting ship, they seemed like an army of crawling insects dragging a bright pinkish tail—the red sun reflecting from minute particles. Eckem Meluq swore, "Rataq's there, the swork, and the Earthians. I know they are there. But that lazy gonfi Ubeq can't find them!" He pounded his fat fist on the chair arm.

Trailing behind in the dust trudged the women and children and the prisoners. All morning they walked in the eye-stinging dust, the clumsy weight of the puno collars growing heavier, more chafing, by the hour. Early in the day all eight had been able to draw together; the youths holding their tethers were watchful but did not control their movements as long as they followed the herd. Their hands were free for the day. They had been given a job to do, and there was no chance for escape, with Sukota on grybins scattered in every direction.

Walking with the women, the prisoners searched for the droppings of the flocks. They scooped up the fresh dung and molded it with their hands into bricks, striding forward from time to time to drop the soft bricks into a cart divided into bins for the different kinds. The magli and the grybin dung burned with more smoke than the others, good when many insects flew. The koano burned hottest, the tipula gave the best flavor to barbecuing meat.

Brian watched Mirren stalking through the beaten-down grass, saw her distorted grimace, head turned to one side, as she formed a mush brick with her white hands. "Someday we can remember and laugh at this," he said.

Mirren wrinkled her nose. "I could laugh right now at the sight of the great redbearded warrior, Brian Boru McCann, messenger from Llu to all the Thana, stooping to pick up wet cowpats, but I am trying to breath as little as possible."

Brian weighed the dung in his hand. "I considered throwing it, but there is no high chief near for a worthy target. There will be better times to fight."

Rataq refused the job. They tied his rope to the dung cart, which then hauled him by his neck like a tethered animal.

Inibek Kob tramped in a seeming daze, stooping from time to time, expressionless eyes staring vacantly.

Brian spoke to him and he answered in a weary voice. "My life is worth no more than one of these droppings. They have destroyed my first companion, they have taken our best wife, they have scattered our family. They have taken Kel-Birat. They have torn out my heart; they have made an emptiness in my breast. We had thought to throw ourselves like lightning on the Sukota, our enemies, but we were only raindrops, little raindrops. Could I but get in front of the koano, I would throw myself under their feet."

Brian was taken aback. Was this sturdy Kovas beaten down so completely? He could not accept it. He scoffed, "You, a powerful man—are you letting a little dust and dung destroy you? Your tribe is not annihilated. Your raid included but a few of your people. Will they not come after you?"

"They have no leader. Our sons are yet children, if they still live. Our cousins will fight each other to be deitch. No one will come. They have destroyed the tent, they have put out the fire. Oveda, my wife, walks here and does not recognize me. I have no wife. I have no tribe. I have no friends, no friends but my shadow, no weapon, no weapon but my fingers." He stared down at his hands, covered with filth.

"We are your friends. If no one comes we will escape. You will again lead your clan."

Inibek shook his head. "Five strangers, two of them women, and two only of my people, prisoners, all doing women's work."

"Nevertheless, if I find a way to unlock your collar in secret, so that we have a chance, will you escape?"

Inibek's eyes focused. He stopped and peered at Brian. "If you do that I am your brother, your ordun. I will escape." His hands squeezed hard. Tipula dung oozed between his fingers into the black fur on the backs of his hands.

In the late evening they made a temporary camp on the open steppe. The prisoners, hands locked again in their collars after the day's march, sat on the ground in the midst of toiling confusion.

Except for those guarding the flocks, the men unloaded materials for a quick camp from the tipulas and carts—hair and reed mats for windbreaks, hides for groundcloths, iron tripods for cooking. It was a dry camp. They gave drink only to the working animals, guams and tipula, from the leather water skins. It was another day's trek to water for the herds. They would be restless through the night.

Xergin's and Togrel's women braced up some mattings against the wind, made fires, and set up two tripods. The men slaughtered two magli and stripped the meat from the bones. They cleaned out the paunches of the animals, tied them with rawhide strips to the tripod legs. Into these stomach linings the women poured water, added sliced-up tubers, a kind of wild yoka they had gathered along the way with their digging sticks, and the meat of the magli. They added, too, seasoning herbs from the soft leather pouches they wore at their waists. They enlarged the little fires with the bones of the animals, and heated fist-sized stones to put in the paunches to boil the stew. Ecological efficiency, Brian thought; they make the beasts boil themselves.

Brian noticed particularly one mature woman, the one he had seen with the Sukota when they first captured him. Other women came and went, milked the mesors and magli, did camp chores, but she remained close by the fires in the lee of the mattings. She was taller than the other women and walked with a presence, stood gazing into the fire with the solid dignity of a clean-shafted pine tree, heedless of the prisoners nearby. The fire cast orange tints on the beige of her body fur as she began to stir through the long neck of a leather bag with a narrow wooden paddle. Her black-furred face was calm, her lips firmly set, her multifaceted eyes looked only at her work or at the fire she tended, adding occasionally a heated rock to the boiling stew. All her movements were mechanical, her attention seeming far away at another camp, another time.

Seeing the tightly drawn face of Inibek gazing at her, Brian knew who she was.

"You don't speak to her?" Brian asked.

Numbly he answered, "They watch, they watch. They have directed her to appear here. If she shows any feeling for me, they will kill. This was her tribe. Benjak and I took her from here."

"Took her? By force?"

"By force. How else? Now returned, she is already given by Xergin to Pukar, chief of a subtribe. They test her. They watch. I cannot talk to her. She is mother of my children and Benjak's, but I cannot talk to her. To her I am poison. To her I am like the fangs of a stril." His great shoulders sagged, his hooded eyes stared at the ground.

"But when we escape," Brian whispered.

"Yes, when we do." His back straightened a little. He raised his eyes.

Brian had made his point. He changed the subject. "Why do we make this long move? The camp was pleasant by the river. They had only to shift a little way up the river to get rid of the refuse."

"They are good leaders, Xergin and Togrel, they know pasture."

"What do you mean, know pasture?"

"Grasses are mixed. Koano eat certain kinds. Magli like more kinds than grybins and tipula, and they crop it closer. With too long a stay in one place, the magli eat the good grasses to the roots and bad grass takes over. They keep the herds mixed and move in time." His eyes never left

Oveda by the fire.

"What is she stirring?"

"It is kukri," said Inibek. "Fermented grybin's milk. After a thirsty day they will drink much. They will sleep heavy."

The cutting wind blew more strongly. The Sukota drew closer to their many fires. Oveda left the kukri standing in its stiff leather sack and returned shortly, wearing a soft magli cape pinned at the shoulder with a large red brooch.

Inibek Kob kept his face expressionless as he whispered to Brian, "That stone I took from a Vanth lord in a raid many nins ago. A skilled artisan made the pin and set the stone. She tells me she remembers."

The thought of the long pin fathered an idea in Brian's mind. It could be a way to pick the locks of the collars. They were heavy wrought iron but simple in design.

He spoke softly. "If you can get Oveda to let us have that brooch, I can unlock the collars."

Kob sucked breath noisily through his teeth. "I cannot speak to her or go near. But my children are her children, she may drop her brooch nearby if you tell her I wish it. But let no one see you speak."

Brian began slowly to wander about the camp. His shoulders were raw, bleeding from marching over rough ground all day under the jerking weight of the wooden collar. His neck felt as if it were broken, with the splintered bone ends grinding against each other whenever he moved, but still he wandered. The boy holding his check rope went along easily enough; Brian was making no attempt to leave the camp.

He paused by four women sitting around a large tanned hide spread on the grass, beating with sticks the hair sheared from the two magli before they were slaughtered. "To soften it," one answered his question. "Then we wet it again and roll it tight between reed mats. Tomorrow it rides on the cart. Evening we pound it again. After many dohls like that we dry it in the yann."

"Then it is a tent covering?"

They agreed, nodding.

Sheltered from the wind by one of the carts, he saw two other women sitting together beside a cradle of wood strips, bent and secured with rawhide to make a cage. The babe could not fall out. Brian smiled. The baby smiled back. Brian wandered on.

His roamings finally brought him back close to Oveda, where she was in the act of lifting the bag of kukri to carry it to the men who waited. As he passed by her, his back toward the men and his guard, he whispered low, "You can save Inibek by dropping your brooch beside me."

Brian was sure she had heard, but she gave no sign, nor did he expect any. His answer, if any, would come later. He had done what he could. Now it depended on her, a wife stolen and restolen. She could not know nor understand how much turned on her action, the dropping or not dropping of a prized jewel in the dust.

Brian squatted beside Inibek and tried to ease his aching neck. Maybe it did not really matter. Even if they loosed their collars, could they get away from pursuit? Could Rataq make his contact? Could they ever really do anything? Meluq, Ubeq and Barsorq had a clear field, had everything.

He felt old and small and as helpless as a pebble lying in the midst of the endless steppe crushed into the dirt by a koano hoof.

"I have told her. Will she?"

"She will. She must, she must."

Brian caught the note of pleading. Inibek was not sure. He watched Oveda lift the weighty leather sack. Pukar had beckoned to her, waving his drinking cup of wobargu horn over the fire before him. He sat on a hide beside Xergin and Togrel. Each leaned against the warm belly of his Kel-grybin, Kel-Ufar and Kel-Segan. Pukar had Kel-Birat picketed nearby. It would be many nins before she would lie down for a new master.

Brian nudged Inibek. "Kel-Birat?"

"I know," he spat. "He will die for that."

Brian grinned. He's getting his spirit back, he thought. He watched Oveda fill cups with kukri—many cups, many times. After awhile he lay down near Inibek Kob. When finally Oveda returned to the fire to set down the empty sack, Brian was tense as a stretched spring. Now was her opportunity.

She stooped to add dung to the fire, then rose and stalked away.

Brian's spring was about to snap. Nothing. Then he caught sight of a red gleam in the dust by the fire. He rolled over, not quickly, just casually, to be closer to the fire for the night, but he made sure the brooch was under his side. Their young guards were already half asleep. With the lines to the collars tied to their wrists, no one could run without causing alarm.

Brian waited, waited while the fire died again, waited for camp activity to quiet down, waited for Xergin and Pukar to settle for sleep. While he waited he worked his body backward slowly until the circle of the brooch pressed into his shoulder as he lay on his side. The cold wind whipped around and through the matting windbreak, raising fluttering sounds in the reeds, and reached in through numbed muscles to chill his bones. But his thoughts were heated, racing ahead. Get rid of the collars, steal grybins. Ride, ride. Get Mirren and Ngora safely to a Kiyatagu camp. Then it would be time for Cogbard to be arriving at the plateau to bring news of the Litanofoq. Kiyatagu guarding at the head of the red gate would bring him in. All this tribal raiding was a distraction. He could get back to the main problem.

The camp was quieting down. Sukota wrapped in their cloaks lay between their fires and their windbreaks. Two Sukota women appeared, picked up the tethers fastened to the collars of Mirren and Ngora, jerked them up. Stiff with the long day's trek and the cold, stumbling, they were led away. They disappeared beyond a cluster of screens. Brian saw Mirren's face, a white shape in the dark, looking toward him. Then she was gone.

Brian's racing thoughts collapsed. He groaned. Could he wait until the next night when they might be together again? But the pattern would repeat. They would be separated long before the camp was quiet enough to make a try. Delay would only endanger escape. The brooch might be missed. He might be searched. Better tonight. He would have to find where they went.

Xergin and Togrel rose from their comfortable seats against their grybins, yawned and stretched. Pukar lay snoring, mouth open. Xergin toed his ribs. He moaned and stirred, but he did not wake. He had swallowed a great deal of kukri. Xergin kicked again, harder. Still he did not move. Xergin shrugged. He and Togrel, their kel-grybins following them like dogs, walked off toward the screen where Ulfilas lay with their three children.

Trying to ease his tortured neck clamped in the anchor of the puno collar, Brian worked his body lower. Now the iron circle of the brooch lay above his shoulder beside the collar. Also he lay head to head with Inibek. Now their own guards and the camp seemed asleep, save for the few watchmen who rode about the flocks nearby, calling to each other in subdued voices, not talk, not song, but something in between, a quiet lulling sound reassuring to the animals that all was well.

Whispered instructions brought the heads of the group together—six of them—like spokes of a wheel. Brian humped himself up on his knees to bring his right hand, his wrist pinioned by the collar, close to the brooch. Almost he stood on his head to finally grasp it.

He elbowed himself to reach the lock on Kob's collar. He pried in the simple lock with the long pin of the brooch. A loud snap like the crack of doom sounded in his ear, the end of the iron pin breaking off. He collapsed to the ground, lay still. Did anyone hear? The tether holder closest to him stirred in his sleep.

## nine

When all was quiet again, Brian fingered out the broken piece, the end of the iron pin.

"Broke?" whispered Kob.

"What's left is thicker. Maybe it's still long enough."

The lock was large and heavy and not lubricated, but at least it was a simple lock, held by friction alone; there was no spring. He pried in the hole to push up the single tumbler. It moved a little. He nudged it along some more. With the next thrust it let go.

Kob slipped one hand out of his collar to release Brian, and one by one, laboriously, each released the next beside him, keeping within the limits of their ropes. They lay in place with collars in position, hands touching around the circle, until all were ready.

They lay quiet—Brian, Kob, Kors, Rataq and two of Kob's Kiyatagu. They listened. The sounds of the night seemed louder than before. The wind over the camp carried both sounds and smells he had scarcely noticed, rustlings of restless sleepers, rattling as the wind fussed at the reed mattings, a soft hiss as a coal of the dying fire broke apart. Vagrant sounds came from the herd of grybins and their guards, upwind from the camp. Smells too came from the herd, and faint smells of cooking not yet totally dissipated, and smells of unwashed Kovas bodies, and above all the dry smell of the grass.

A guard walked among them suspiciously. They lay still, controlling their breathing. The guard kicked Inibek in the ribs.

Brian heard the derisive laugh like a ragged edged cough. He felt Inibek's wire-tense fingers scrape and dig in the dirt. Brian poured all his attention and consciousness into willing Kob not to move. If he reached, if he hauled him down, the Sukota would wake the camp before he died.

Inibek lay as dangerous as an armed missile. A muffled oath escaped his lips, but he lay still.

The guard walked on unaware.

An animal's cough sounded from a distance, borne on the wind—a grating, savage kind of a cough, strange to Brian. "What is that?" He looked toward Inibek. In the dark all he could see was the myriad tiny pinpoints of red light, the low glimmer of fire reflecting from his eyes.

"Hunting klugon," Inibek whispered. "It will frighten the herds. Confusion will help us. The time is now!"

"Tula and Radja, kill the grybin guards. All get mounts and remounts. Stampede the rest. I'll be with you in moments."

Careful not to tug on their tethering ropes, they opened their collars, rose silently and crept away from the fire. Brian hesitated. Should he look first for Mirren and Ngora or get a mount and then find them? He followed Kob toward the center of the camp.

He saw Kob creep to the snoring Pukar. Roughly he jerked the knife from Pukar's belt. Pukar started up, calling, "What, wha...." and ended with a choking gurgle. Kob had slit his throat. There was no other sound; no one stirred. Kel-Birat sniffed at Inibek and snorted softly. Kob quickly laid his hand on her nose.

Brian continued beyond Kob, searching, trying in the dark to distinguish if any figure lying there wore a wooden collar. The thick darkness seemed almost solid. He saw nothing except where still glowing coals showed an arm or leg in a dim circle of light. Soon he was sure to step on someone. He needed Kors. Kors' eyes saw in infrared. Kors could find them.

Brian turned back, hurrying toward where he had last seen Kors. Suddenly there was someone beside him in the dark, someone leading a grybin.

It was Rataq. "Got one! Here, hold his head while I mount."

Brian took the rope halter. Rataq jumped to lie across its back, swing a leg around to sit astride. In the midst of his motion the grybin bucked. Its loud snort was almost a scream. Brian hung on, trying to soothe the animal. Rataq landed in the dirt.

Around them, sleepers stirred, barked questions.

Inibek, on Kel-Birat, loomed in the blackness. "Mount quickly," he whispered. Then he recognized the Kel-grybin. "Ho, Kel-Ufar, Xergin's steed." Swiftly he tied a rope to the halter.

Rataq started to mount again.

"No, no. He will not permit. First you must make friends with a Kel-grybin. But we will take her."

In another moment Brian found Kors, and they turned back toward the camp that now was buzzing. Shouts were heard, torches being lit.

Inibek stopped them. "We go."

"I must find Mirren and Ngora!" Brian ran toward the camp. Kob pursued, baring the sword he had taken from Pukar. He smote Brian on the back of the head with the flat of it.

"Kors, get him on a grybin. We'll get the women another time."

In his dimly returning consciousness Brian felt only stabbings of pain; one stab knifed into the back of his head. Another he felt through his haze from his body, his body that was vaguely down below his head somewhere with the agony knifing up through it. He struggled to lift his hand to touch the back of his head. Both arms were held. The pain in his body grew clearer now. It was a pounding in his groin. He tried to scream, but only moans came from his lips.

"He's coming round," someone said.

Brian tried to turn off his consciousness to balk the pain, but only increased his awareness. He opened his eyes. He was riding on a grybin without a pad saddle, bareback. He was held upright by Tulu on one side, Radja on the other. That was riding skill, to race through the night holding a man on his mount between them. The pounding pain was the shoulder blades of the running grybin working under him, pounding. Quarks, no wonder they use thick pad saddles.

Finally his voice worked. "Walk! Let's walk!" He shook his arms loose. In the lead, Inibek looked back, slowed to a halt.

"All walk, rest grybins," Inibek called.

Brian slid off. He wondered were they all hurting; they all rode bareback. But, conscious, they could adjust their seats behind the working shoulders without moving far enough back to injure a grybin's spine.

Inibek Kob clapped Brian on the shoulder. "Take them time to catch mounts. Take them longer time to find where our tracks separate from herd's. Soon we reach last water before desert. It is better not to be too far in the lead. If they chase all across the desert, our people watch water holes on our side." A grin formed on the dark rugged face. He was feeling a man again. He gripped Brian's arm. "I will remember," he said.

With one arm slung over the grybin's back, Brian began to walk, staggering at first but gradually gaining control. He chained his thought to placing one foot before the other to keep his attention away from the slashes of pain.

The sun's red glow was spreading above the mountains toward the east, but they plodded on in the shadows of a valley. He could hear the chatter of a small stream in a rocky bed beyond the thick blackness of a fringe of trees and undergrowth. He sniffed at the smell of moisture in the fresh morning air. They were again traversing the wide depression at the foot of the mountains. If he did not hurt, it could have been an invigorating morning ride.

But Mirren! Ngora!

Realization flooded back through his mind. He put his hand up to feel the back of his head. There was a lump, the covering hair matted with dried blood.

"Who bashed me on the head?"

Inibek turned, grinning. "It was I who saved you."

Brian shouted, "You stopped me from going for Mirren!" Blood pounded in his head. It felt ready to explode out the back. He reached for his sword but it was not there. The Sukota had taken it.

Kob laughed. "You were stubborn, and you have a hard head. You are worth saving. It takes time to make a man, and there are many other women."

"That's not my way!"

"Well, maybe among your kind there is a problem. You can settle it at the gathering. Here." He removed the sword he wore and tossed it to Brian.

"This is your great sword. I found it lying beside Pukar."

Brian caught the scabbard with his left hand and snatched out the sword with his right. His eyes burned with anger.

Inibek stood, saying no word.

Suddenly Brian had a vision of himself threatening a motionless unarmed man, the one who a moment before had given him the sword. He resheathed it. "I'll go back for her," he mumbled.

"Your head is so hard it can take another blow?"

Behind him, Brian heard Rataq. "I'll go with you. We must retrieve Ngora from her captivity."

Brian felt a surge of good will toward Rataq. He was proving a good companion in the wars. Maybe his doubts were mistaken.

Kob continued, "Do not be foolish. The hive has been poked up. The gavies are buzzing about looking for someone to sting. There is a better way. In a little while, one nin only, comes the gathering. There you can fight for her—each of you can fight for your own." His tone and face were full of friendly feeling. "No hurry now. Whatever is done is done. Whatever is not done is not done."

"Blast! I must go now. Waiting is no good. We will go at night, lay up in the daytime."

Inibek pulled at his lip. "Maybe when the hive has not been disturbed you could that, but now the hive is all buzz buzz. The gavies are wild. They will miss no one coming close to the hive. You throw yourself away. At the Nyada you can do battle."

Brian grunted, "You may be right, but a man ought to do what a man can do. You stopped me once. I don't thank you for that."

"You can thank me you are still alive."

Rataq spoke. "Swar Kob has the right of it. Getting ourselves trussed up again in wooden collars or meeting our deaths would help no one.

Let us wait for the Nyada."

They are right, Brian thought. But it felt wrong. He was not free; his first purpose was still to get the *Plymouth* safely down. He had to stick with the slim chance with Rataq, not switch to no chance at all.

Inibek slapped Rataq on the back. "Lazo Rataq, you did a great thing when you took Xergin's Kel-Ufar. Ho, he will rip your head off your neck if he catches you. We will tell of it at campfires."

Rataq stumbled under the blow and reached for his blaster, but nothing was there. "You beat me at great risk." His voice was hot.

Kob laughed. "I really beat you and you know the difference. Now I will tell you about Kel-grybins." He looped the rope lead to Kel-Ufar in his hand until the grybin walked at his shoulder, beside Rataq. Kel-Birat followed at his other shoulder without a line.

"A Kel-grybin permits only his master on his back. You must teach Kel-Ufar you are his master. But first you must make friends." He patted and rubbed the jaw of Kel-Birat. He fondled the soft skin of the nose, and the animal's mobile lips responded.

Rataq imitated with Kel-Ufar. She jerked up her head, bared her teeth.

Kob spoke in soothing tones and, with gentle pressure, pulled the head down again. "It takes time. And you must learn to read the ears. If they point ahead, they tell you what she notices. Pricked sharply forward, she is greatly interested. Just now, when she jerked her head, did you see her ears turn down and back? If her lips are tight, ears drooping, eye folds half over her eyes, she is unhappy. If her teeth are bared, nostrils pinched tight, ears flat back, she tells you she is angry—her bite crunches, her kick crushes.

"She does not understand your words, but she learns your voice. She hears your anger, your love. She feels your hands. She knows your fear, your confidence, and when you are astride, she feels all these through her skin. Kel-grybins are smart grybins. She wants a quiet easy life, plenty of food and drink, and if she does not respect you, she knows many tricks to keep out of work. She slouches, neck drooping, looks tired all over. She will heave a great sigh when you throw on the saddle pad. You will think she is all worn out. But if she learns to respect you, if you love her and train her, she will want to please you. She will carry you all day, all night, and never another grybin can catch her."

It was daylight when they watered and rested briefly at the pool by the ribbon of waterfall, the last water before the desert. Brian sat on the same brown monzonite boulder where he had first learned he was part of a raid on the Sukota. Only five were left of the more than fifty companions he had had then. He gazed up the desolate channel of a valley that here veered east toward the mountains before it swung north again. His weary eyes scanned the dark jagged line of peaks. He tried to relax away from pain, to hold the idea of calm water, the quiet coolness of moisture in the air. He attempted to draw out the resting to a greater length of time, by concentration to be aware now of time, and turn time off when again they rode.

His eyes caught a glint from one of the mountain peaks, bright with a flash of red, brighter than anything so far away could possibly be. He was sure it was the same light he had noted once before at sunset. Turning to Inibek, he pointed.

"What peak is that?"

Inibek followed his extended arm. "That is altar dumo of Runn. In the valley beside it will be the

Dormala, in another 30 dhols."

Brian translated, "The gathering at great fire throne mountain."

"The light speaks from Altar Runn, the seat of the lord, the throne of Nalpur of Runn."

Brian wondered again what caused the gleaming redness. The light had not been there during the night; it was certainly no volcano.

On the road again, Inibek Kob saw the air car first, but he did not know what it was. Already it was close over them when he cried out in wonder. "What is that that flies and follows?"

Rataq knew and Brian knew. Was it going to be captivity again, a far tougher one to break out of?

The stubby shining metallic cylinder hovered above, searching. They pulled the hoods of their capes lower, kept their heads down. Did they all look like Thana-Kovas? Could the Litani pick them out? Their disguise had to hold up. There was no way to run.

All the Kovas stared upward. The two lowered heads were the betrayal.

The cylinder swept forward and settled to the valley floor. Landing skids supported it just off the ground. Brian and Rataq exchanged glances. "Watch for a chance," Brian said softly from the corner of his mouth.

The Kovas waited warily. Two Litanofoq stepped down, black, the Q family. Each held a blaster in his fist. One was Terko Ubeq. The yellow face of a third appeared in the open doorway. Round faces, rounded foreheads, round noses with bridges sloping to nothing between round black eyes. Faces of aged children wreathed in savage grins of triumph.

Rataq stepped forward. "They want us. Will you care for Kel-Ufar until I return?"

Kob jerked the lead rope from Rataq, his face grim, his voice accusing. "You are one of these people? This Brian McCann is also? Now I know you come from another world, from the world of the gods or the world of the dead. There are no other worlds. Which is it? What do you want from us? And I was teaching you about Kel-grybins! Do you help us, or do you destroy us?"

Brian gripped Inibek's shoulder. With great sincerity he said, "You have helped us, and we still need help from you, but Llu and Nalpur of Runn willing, we mean to return to you value full and overflowing."

Rataq was silent facing the Litani, his eyes calculating.

With his blaster Terko beckoned Rataq. "Come now," he barked. "You too." He waved his blaster toward Brian.

At least they are not going to shoot us down right here, Brian thought.

Rataq spoke to Brian in Earthian. "The pilot in the doorway is one of us. He will take care of the one nearest him if we move."

Brian concentrated on Terko Ubeq. Did he understand?

"No more talk," Terko yelled. His eyes darted back and forth between Rataq and Brian.

The two with the blasters were stepping away from the door, one to either side. In a moment both would be beyond the reach of the pilot.

Rataq screamed a wordless scream. Both whipped their blasters toward him.

Brian leaped, smashed down Ubeq's arm. The sand at Rataq's feet bubbled into molten glass. The pilot belted the back of the other one's head with something metallic in his fist. Brian's fist smashed into Terko's little round nose. He wrenched away the blaster.

Inibek Kob and his men looked on with puzzled faces during the entire thirty-five seconds of the action. Brian helped Rataq load the two limp bodies. They faced each other at the doorway, Rataq in the air car, Brian on the ground.

"This is great! We can go for Mirren and Ngora in this!"

"Yes indeed." Rataq now wore a triumphant grin. "In two days I will return for that purpose. Now I must fly back to Colufo. This is too fine an opportunity to neglect. I will see that my people are organized and alerted for a takeover."

"Then I should come too, and Kors. We can coordinate with the Thana."

"I would like to take you, but I must go as secretly as possible. You are much too large, too tall to be disguised. The Thana we will take care of later."

He slid the door shut, and the air car shot up silently before Brian could say more. He stood perplexed. That was a mighty quick-and-easy battle. Rataq flew away from here in a terrible hurry, and he made it a point to leave me behind. Was this whole thing a setup? Earlier when he took off into the desert, was he unworried because he expected Terko to come pick him up? And we were in trouble only because Terko was late? Still, why such a setup? To get us away from Colufo? We might have organized some opposition there. But here, separated, among strangers. . . . But maybe he is just excited, eager to get back in touch. Maybe he really will be back in two days.

Brian watched the air car speed away over the red cliffs. His gaze dropped along the dark stains that drifted down the cliffs—marks of mineral-laden dripping water—to the base where white sand had blown up into sloping crevices and shelves like white surf frozen there against the dark rock of the shore, never returning to the sea of sand.

## ten

Two long, hard-riding days later the desert phased gradually to short scattered tufts of grass, then to longer and longer grasses growing closer, until the world grew gray-green around the travelers, and the dry dusty smell of sun-parched grass puffed up around them from beating grybin hooves. All day Brian watched the sky. By the time they reached the first tiny stream that trickled down from the higher mountains, he felt sure Rataq was false. He had succeeded in scattering the Earthians: the women were captive in one corner of the high plains, Brian fled from capture in another, and Kors, who would have been the most effective leader of the Thana, was with him. But Rataq could not know that. It was a bonus. Still, it was a wild way to get rid of his opposition. He could have taken over by brute force, he had the power. Brian shook his head in puzzlement as he scanned the sky.

There was little hope without Rataq. How could Brian alone, with the survivors of a desperate tribal raid, do anything to prevent the Litanofoq from wiping out the *Plymouth* and everybody in it before they had any warning at all?

At last in one midafternoon, Inibek pulled Kel-

Birat to a halt where their way slanted down beside a roistering stream dashing itself into white spray against the rocks that fought to hold back its downward rush. Brian breathed deep of the cheering smell of moisture. He dismounted quickly, splashed cold water over his head and face.

Inibek Kob sat with the folds around his eyes pulled together against the wind, gazing down into the wide expanse of green valley that spread out before them.

"Brian McCann with the far-seeing eyes, what do you see? Are there herds in the valley—koana, tipula, magli? Are there torkas by the stream?"

Brian followed his gaze down the valley, where the stream ceased its rushing to wander quietly across the floor between curving green banks. "I see groups of little black dots; I see, scattered along the river, many round gray mushrooms that are torkas."

"Yes, good, good." Inibek nodded. "I hoped they might be here before us. The grass on the lower steppe is dry by now. Good grass here will last several dhols; then there are higher mountain valleys on the way to Dormala. But is there a torka that is black?"

Brian peered again toward the valley floor. "Yes, there is one torka that is black."

Inibek sighed a long sigh. "It is as I feared."

There was aging in his face that Brian had not noticed before. There was gray in the black fur of his cheeks. His eyes were weary and dull, his great shoulders sagged.

"We crawl back like beaten werfs—three of us, of the fifty who rode, and two strangers. Little we have accomplished. Benjak is not avenged. We thought to plunge down on our enemies like a fast-breaking storm, but it was our own blood that wet the ground. We come back lower than the gao who slithers on the ground." His sigh raised his massive chest. "Still we live. Now we go to prepare the dead."

The sound of the wailing carried to them on the wind long before they reached the black torka. An empty wagon was drawn up some little distance away, but nothing else had been done to make ready. Kob's three brothers and Benjak's single brother were lost in the raid. There were no women in the household—some servants, but no wives. Oveda was with the Sukota. Three others had disappeared. The more distant kinsmen, cousins among the remaining members of the tribe, were hesitant about assuming leadership. It could be dangerous should Inibek Kob return.

Two boys and a girl rushed to Inibek. Alungo, the younger boy, about nine gatherings in age, and Oarda, the girl, still younger, flung their arms about Inibek's hips.

"Mommy—did you find Mommy?"

The older boy, Ekai, tall and lean, hung back, hesitating, self-conscious, until Inibek beckoned and drew him in beside the others.

"I found her. She is all right. But I could not bring her back." His voice was husky. He straightened up, cuffed each one gently on the shoulder. "Now we have a job to do." He waved toward the black torka.

Ekai asked, "Where are all the others?"

Inibek opened his mouth to speak, then closed it, saying nothing. He nodded toward Tuli and Radja.

"In three gatherings I will be big enough. I will not forget." Ekai squared his shoulders, turned and walked away, stumbled, recovered and continued.

Alungo clung to his father's hand. "Tell us what happened," he begged.

Inibek was silent for a long pause; finally he

said, "Yes, it is right you should know. But not now, later. Now we have a duty to perform."

Now Kob, grim faced, gave orders. The wailing ceased. Funeral preparations gathered speed. Wood was dragged down from nearby heights, enough yearling koana and magli were slaughtered for the assembled tribe, kukri was fermented. Benjak's body was eviscerated and filled with dried grass and the special tengri herbs that burned hot with a sharp-smelling fragrance. By the end of the second day, wrapped in his best softened koana-hide cloak decorated with swirling red and black stripes and edged with wobargo fur, and belted with sword belt and sword, Benjak lay on the fur-piled bed frame in the black torka, ready.

Inibek Kob stood alone eying the prepared body. Suddenly he swung about, strode out of the hut. Outside, he shouted. Tribesmen gathered in the purpling dusk. Angrily he spoke. "There is no wife. Would you have the deitch of the Kiyatagu approach the Nalpur of Runn beyond the curtains of the night unattended by a worthy and respectful helpmeet? Where is the pride of the Kiyatagu? Has our clan no dignity? Are we without honor? Do we cringe like beaten werfs, chittering in the dark?"

Humbly, Girta, one of the cousins, spoke. "With all respect, Deitch Inibek Kob, the wives fled during the Sukota raid. We do not know where they are."

Kob's stare turned fierce. "False one! There is a decorated robe bound about Benjak's body. Only the wives keep and guard the decorated robes. There was a wife here until he died." He gazed man by man at the gathering. "So they are scattered and hiding. You are Kiyatagu. You are like hawks in the sky. You range far. You see everything that moves on the grass. You will find wives. You will bring them here!"

Inibek jabbed with stiff forefinger into the chest of Girta. "You will search. You will find. You will bring wives here." He paused, then added softly, slowly, "Or you, Girta, poorly equipped as you are for the honor, will be strangled to take her place." He gazed around at the gathered figures. "Perhaps it may require more than one to fill her place adequately. You have until the yann is noon high tomorrow."

Girta held himself stiff under the threat. "It shall be as you say."

Next morning, after a breakfast of loggets and mesor milk, Brian stepped out of the torka. The blood-red yann had just cleared the rim of the mountains in the east. In the distance toward the west, Brian saw three riders approaching. Soon he recognized Cogbard, escorted by two Kiyatagu. There would be news!

Brian eyed Cogbard as he dismounted and swaggered forward. Already he had his brush out and was cleaning the dust from the thick black fur of his arms and face. Striding toward Brian, he rotated his huge shoulders one after the other, shrugging off the weariness of the long ride. He gazed at Brian with bold staring eyes, catlike ears pricked up at a cocky angle, the wings of his widespreading nostrils working, his thick curling lips pulled down at the corners in a fierce look.

Kors came up beside Brian. Their eyes met. *Cogbard is overdoing it. Something is bothering him, and Kors sees it too,* Brian thought.

Cogbard's first words were barked. "Where's Rataq?"

"Gone to Colufo in an air car," Kors answered.

Cogbard's eyes were puzzled. "They came for him?"

Kors laughed. "Well, not exactly."

Cogbard ignored it. "Where are the others, the

women?"

"They are with another tribe. Come, first companion—as they say here." He laid his hand on Cogbard's arm. "You are tired and hungry from the long ride. I will find food, and you will tell news."

As he left, Cogbard's eyes lingered on Brian. "The only one here," he muttered.

Brian felt the look, shook his head. Something was unnatural. He followed to hear news of the Thana.

Cogbard told them that the Litani were good people. "Why should they not be good people? Are they not descendents of the Old Litani returned to their home? Are they not brothers, big brothers? They will teach us many good things," he said.

"How do the Thana in Colufo get along with the Litanofoq?" Brian asked.

"Well, there are no Thana in Colufo any more. They had to move out into camps in the fields to let the Litani live in the houses. You see the Litani cannot live in the open, they are used to living closed in their great ship in the sky. But they are good people. And more and more they are going out in the streets, too."

"And what of Tsankta?"

"Well, Litani are living there too. They held us prisoner for awhile, but they let me go. They are good people."

"Tavita a prisoner? We go to Tsankta now!"

"No, no, not now. She is not really a prisoner. But they take good care of her."

Kors looked past Cogbard to Brian. His face was troubled. "Something is wrong."

Brian thought he knew what it was. But he just said, "We can do nothing alone. When Rataq returns. . . ."

"He is overdue."

That day the Kel-grybin of Benjak, Kel-Nirza, was fed a last meal of hearty grain, and in the midst of it she was suddenly spiked through the forehead, a quick death. Her belly was cleaned out, then stuffed with straw and tengri herbs, and closed again. A stake was driven through her lengthwise, and she was propped on the two halves of a wheel that were held upright in tandem by thick posts.

Benjak's most elaborately decorated pad saddle, stuffed with tipula hair, was strapped in place on Kel-Nirza. It glowed a lustrous red, with bright white figures of koana and tipula sewn with bold stitches of leather strips to the hanging leather skirts. From the single bridle rein hung red leather cutouts of savage klugon heads, and from the tips of the grybin's upstanding horns hung red tassels. It was a gay colorful display for a staked-up dead grybin. Brian wondered what came next.

Next it was the wagon drawn close beside the Kel-grybin, the guams spiked and lying in place beside the wagon tongue. On the wagon lay a woman, her face contorted in agony with the expression frozen by death, the wife who was needed to accompany Benjak. Girta had been busy during the night. Brian was glad he had been asleep. It was better that he not interfere in tribal customs. At her feet lay a man servant for attendance on both Benjak and his wife. Piled around them were all their necessaries, spear and sword, baskets of dried meat, loggets and yoka, clay pots and dishes, a bag of kukri, extra robes and furs— all a man should need for his comfort when making a long journey.

Then came the final act of preparation. Benjak was carried out from the blackened torka and mounted on his Kel-Nirza. A stake driven upward through his body was fitted down through Kel-

Nirza's back into the hole in the horizontal bar that ran lengthwise through the grybin. Now the wood was piled around grybin and wagon. Branches and leaves of the fragrant burning bush, the tengri, were strewn throughout the faggots, covering the half wheels and the legs of Kel-Nirza. She stood with her master on her back ready to ride on wings of flame to the world of the dead.

In the short time of the return of Inibek Kob, word had spread. A growing stream of men of the tribe rode in to swear allegiance to Inibek, deitch of the Kiyatagu, and to urge him to accept another first companion, so that the two remaining wives could become fruitful for the increase of the tribe. The valley now held swarms of flocks and the river was lined with torkas.

In the evening, when the torch was applied to the funeral pyre of Benjak, men of the tribe were there in their hundreds. As the flames spread and grew, heavy smoke and the scented vapors from the tengri herbs drifted along the ground.

The tribesmen mounted their grybins, each with his most colorful pad saddle and robe. With Inibek in the lead and Kors beside him, because Kors had been ordun to Benjak, they began slowly to ride in a great circle around the fire, lifting their faces into the smoke, breathing of it deeply. As they rode they began to chant, and the drumming of the grybin hooves wove a rhythm under the song.

> *Our Benjak goes to stay*
> *with the great rider of the wind*
> *with Nalpur the Beneficent*
> *with Nalpur of Runn.*
>
> *Our Benjak, carry for us these messages.*
> *Let us find always*
> *water and grass in plenty.*

*Let the cold time be short
and let the hot time be short,
but the times between,
let them last as long
as the mountains last
and the rivers run.*

*In the hunt
make our arrows fly straight
our spears drive true.
In war
make our arrows fly straight
our lances sink deep
and the battles be won.*

*Oh, Benjak, carry these messages
to the great rider of the wind
to Nalpur the giver of light
to Nalpur of Runn.*

Inibek waved Brian and Cogbard to join the circle. Mounted, they entered. The circle moved faster now. They breathed the clear cool air on the windward, and in the lee the sweetly sharp smoke that stung in their nostrils.

After a few circuits Brian no longer noticed the sting. He felt better than he had in many days. The ache in his neck and groin were gone and his shoulders felt fine.

The pace of the trotting grybins quickened. Brian loved the motion. He wanted to push faster, faster. Cogbard's face lit up with a happy grin. One corner of Brian's mind shrieked, Caution, caution, the smoke is drugging you! He ignored it. He laughed aloud. He kicked his grybin into a run. All the grybins were running, all out. He yelled, "Go it, go it, Cogbard, yeaaah!" Pounding hooves beat grass into dirt. Dust rose into the smoke. "Ride, ride!" Grybin mouths gaped, nostrils flared.

Thana-Kovas nostrils flared, yells, yelling all around, yowls, howls, hooting, whooping, shouts, screams, screeching, bellowing, roaring—no words, just frenzied sound.

They rode, they rode until the grybins too began to stagger. They slowed; the shouting twisted into hysterical laughter. Kovas whacked each other on the shoulders, the back. One Kovas, shaking with manic hilarity, reeled from his saddle, rolled in the dust. Laughter redoubled. Showing how he did it, others collapsed onto the ground.

Women, who had remained to windward beyond the circling grybins, came silently to lead away the riderless mounts.

Brian rolled in a tangle with Cogbard, unable to get to his feet. His head had a happy buzz. Kors and Inibek sat near them, rocking back and forth to some inward rhythm. The four wrapped their arms around each other, attempting to rise. Partway up they lost hold and rolled again in the dirt.

Thumping Cogbard on the chest, Brian cried, "Good ol' Cogbard Ru . . . something un Tsankta, great soldier Cogbard. How, how's. . . ." He forgot what he was going to ask. Nose to nose, they laughed. Kors beat on both their backs.

Cogbard tried to talk. "You know . . . you know what? I am supposed to kill you."

All four laughed and laughed. "He's supposed to kill you," Kors shrieked in laughter.

Brian roared, "Kill, kill, kill."

Inibek howled, "Funniest thing I ever heard, kill."

The head buzzing was fading and Brian was fading with it. "Sleepy," he mumbled, and lay with his head on Cogbard's stomach. Kors' head was on Brian's thigh, Inibek lay across Kors. Heaps of Kovas snored around the still hot-burning fire. The women kept watch to see that no burning ash settled on any of the jumbled slumbering bodies, and they added wood to keep the fire burning hot until morning.

The red sun shone bright in the sky when Brian awoke, cotton brained and soreheaded. He staggered toward the stream to soak his head. There he found Inibek's two wives and three children gouging wet clay out from the bank at the water's edge. Curious, Brian followed them back to the site of last night's funeral fire. As he walked he tried to remember. It was something important, something Cogbard had said last night. He jerked his head in a quick shake. The ache rattled around in it and he groaned.

At the funeral pyre, nothing was left but a fine ash. Rolling their balls of wet clay in the burned-out circle, the women and children kneaded ashes into the clay until there seemed as much ash as clay in their clumps.

Brian watched Ekai and Alungo squatting in the warmth of the morning sun, working their clay. Alungo began, small fingers pushing, pulling, molding. A Kovas on a grybin—Benjak on Kel-Nirza—began to appear in low relief. Beside him, Ekai molded just a head and shoulders. Oarda too worked her clay and ashes. A face was appearing.

Brian lifted his head to Inibek's call. He sniffed the scent floating on the air: hot dolagu. The sharp tang told him he was hungry. At breakfast, Inibek answered his questions. The sun-dried tablets would be votive tablets because Benjak had gone to live with the gods and was now a lesser god than Nalpur, but still a god. The tablets would be taken to the great fire throne mount, Altar Durno Runn, and placed there in a cave below the mountain in memory of the great deitch. In three days now the tribe would begin its move toward the valley called gompani, where the dormala would take place at the foot of Altar Durno Runn.

## eleven

A day of relaxation ought to be a wonderful thing, but Brian's thoughts would not cease their fret. He stood waist deep in a quiet pool, where the stream barely moved between its grassy banks, watching a pair of garlons circle and stoop, glistening silvery wings burnished by the sun. Otherwise the sky was empty. He scrubbed himself with wet sand, grit digging into his skin, ducked under to wash it off, felt scratchy clean. At the sun-warmed surface the water was pleasant; at his feet it was stinging cold. He leaned back to lift his feet and float.

Physically he felt first class, but his problems rasped at his mind like a broken-toothed saw. Mirren and Ngora were still captive. He had done nothing, just run away. The *Plymouth* was fast approaching—it must even now be within easy distance for communication—and what would they receive? Allurements from Colufo, from Rataq maybe. He would know exactly how to call them in. And Brian had done nothing to help there, either. He was far away from the action, outmaneuvered. And there was the important something that Cogbard had said when they were all frazzled out of their minds by the tengri smoke. Brian poked at his memory, but everything after the beginning of that circling ride was fuzzy firelit pictures: Inibek howling a chant into the wind, Kors and Cogbard riding, riding and falling, laughing. Brian splashed water into his face, rubbed his hair and beard, and gave up. If it is important, Cogbard will tell me again, he thought.

Brian shook the water out of his eyes, and there he was, Cogbard, standing on the grassy bank with one foot planted on Brian's ragged some-time white uniform.

Brian eyed him, standing stiffly, tawny fur on his body; black arms, legs and face, erect cat ears, extra broad forehead, enormous multifaceted eyes, jawline slanting down to narrow chin, flaring nostrils of his broad nose. He wore only the typical Thana broad leather belt with one slanting shoulder strap, a pouch hanging in front, a knife in the belt and a great sword at his side. And one hand was slowly drawing it from its heavy scabbard.

Brian's sword lay beside his uniform between Cogbard's feet.

"You were good friend to Thana. You were great warrior to help us against Vanth." Cogbard paused, gazing down at Brian. "Very sorry to do this, but it is necessary."

Brian kicked farther out into the stream. Memory flamed in his brain. "Necessary, my foot! Just why?"

"You are good man for a stranger, but still it is necessary." Cogbard's face was expressionless. He was going to act, not talk.

Brian knew why it was necessary. He knew there was a neat little scar low on the back of Cogbard's head where a micro transponder had been inserted. He was under control. This far from Colufo, he could not be under direct control. He would have been conditioned, instructed and turned loose—

unless there was an air car near. He had asked for
Rataq, Mirren and Ngora, so his instructions were
to kill us all. Rataq! He is to kill Rataq too? Have I
been wrong about Rataq?

Suddenly Brian laughed out loud. Just maybe
Rataq would be returning, and he was the key.
Now he had action. "Okay, Zoto, come get me... if
you can."

Cogbard waded into the stream, holding his
great sword before him.

Brian's mind raced from idea to idea like a
hunting dog quartering a field. There was no place
deep enough where Cogbard could not walk on the
bottom, but he would be clumsy, up to his shoulders
in water. He could not swim; Thana do not like
water. If Brian could draw him far enough from
the bank, then he could roil up the water and swim
past Cogbard under the surface. But the bottom
was coarse clean sand. It wouldn't work. If he
could draw Cogbard far enough then he could
climb out and run for his sword. But Cogbard
always kept between Brian and his clothes.

Brian retreated slowly upstream; Cogbard pursued step by slow step. On the bank now curious
women were gathering, but neither they nor their
men would interfere. This was between two strangers.

The stream began to grow shallow, so Cogbard
could move more freely. Brian would have to take
to the land and run for it. And on land Cogbard
was not slow.

Then Brian saw Kors running. The cavalry had
arrived just in time.

Kors shouted, "Air car coming."

*Quarks! That tears it, Cogbard's control showing
itself. Not the cavalry, just more Indians.*

Kors kept yelling, "Can't hold it off the ground.
It leans, its tail drags." Now he ran at an angle

away from the stream.

"Forget the air car! Get me my sword. My sword!" Brian yelled.

Kors did not turn, eyes on the air car that Brian could not see.

Nuts, he doesn't see what's going on here.

Kors shouted back over his shoulder, "I think it's Rataq."

"Rataq!" Cogbard headed for the riverbank. He leaped out of the water.

Brian swam downstream toward his clothes. Rataq was Cogbard's first target. Forget the sword, no time. Dripping water, Brian dashed after Cogbard and felled him from behind with a hard diving tackle.

Brian jumped up quickly, ready for an onslaught. Cogbard seemed dazed, still on hands and knees with a puzzled look on his face, sword lying beside him. Brian snatched it up.

The air car lurched to a halt before them. Rataq stepped out alone.

"Lazo Rataq! Quarks, am I glad to see you! And you brought an air. . . ." Brian stopped short, sucked in his breath.

Rataq was battered, staggering. His round nose was flattened, the side of his face a massive bruise, one arm hanging limp. As Brian and Kors reached him, he straightened, pointing at Cogbard, only now on his feet.

His words came weakly. "This is Cogbard Rulega an Tsankta. He has been zotoed. He was sent here to slay you and me." He nodded toward the air car. "I have set an interfering signal that will keep him bewildered as long as he is nearby. But he must be restrained."

"He *has* been strange," Brian said, and caught Kors' eye. Kors nodded and helped move Cogbard away, toward the torkas.

Brian gently took Rataq's good arm. "Inibek's women will have food and drink, healing ointments and salves. Later you can tell us what happened."

While both Rataq and Cogbard slept, Brian and Kors talked with Inibek. "Cogbard is first companion," Kors said, "but a spell was cast on him. He is enemy of Brian and Rataq until spell is destroyed."

They agreed that Cogbard would leave early in the morning with an advance party scouting ahead of the trek to begin the next day.

One of Kob's wives smoored the central fire, covering glowing coals with ashes to hold fire until morning, and singing a prayer in a low voice.

*Keep safe the gift of Nalpur*
*this hour, this night and all nights.*
*Keep safe this kargo, this torka, this clan.*


Brian sat by Rataq, dozing at times but always ready to daub a cut with salve or hold another cup of herbal broth to his lips. He should not have doubted. He should not have doubted. But what had happened? Were Rataq's plans all smashed?

Toward morning Rataq roused somewhat, began a half-conscious mumbling. Out of indistinct repetitions, Brian gathered words.

"Outcast . . . leaders imprisoned . . . dead . . . fugitive . . . powerless . . . hunted."

Rataq had been the key. But Rataq was back and the key was broken. Brian felt a great weariness. He rose to creep out of the torka. Outside, he paced along the riverbank. The first hint of dawn, the false dawn, grayed the sky in the east. Darker than gray, shoulders of black mountains loomed, brooding, foreboding. Brian felt alone in an outer darkness between despair and panic.

When the yann was high Brian sat again with Rataq, this time on the grassy riverbank. Behind them, in the many torkas sprinkled along the stream, women tended fires and dried meat and kurds of milk for their trek. Men mended pad saddles, braided rope and prepared other gear for grybins, tipulas and guams.

Rataq's muscles twinged when he moved, but he could move. His greater distress was in spirit. He sat with head bowed toward his drawn-up knees, his answers to Brian little better than groans.

Brian watched drifting muddy pink clouds in a dull blue sky. He breathed deep of the nippy air and pondered how to put some vigor and drive back into Rataq's temper. There must be a way.

Finally, still staring at his feet, Rataq began to talk. "All my effort is wasted—my torture in the desert, almost dying there. My secretly formed organization, my friends on whom I depended, who depended on me—all gone. And what happened to their children? Children are priceless, we have so few."

Brian saw tears well from his eyes, roll down his cheeks. "It can't be that hopeless, truly."

"All of my people dead or imprisoned, maybe zotoed. Eckem Meluq ordered Barsorq and Ubeq to zoto us. Never before have Litani zotoed Litani."

Brian was surprised. "All those centuries on your ship and no operations?"

"Simulated only, to keep skills we would need to zoto the natives when we settled a planet."

Brian said quietly, "Kors is a native. Inibek is a native. Would you zoto them?"

"No, not them, but zotoing assures cooperation."

"To you, Mirren and Ngora would be natives." Brian paused. "You can so consider me also."

"No, no, not you, only those. . . ." He straightened up a little. "It has to be the surest, quickest way."

"Slaves can become unforgiving enemies." Brian waited, hoping for a little fire from Rataq, but he was slumped again. He did not answer.

"Come, let us walk a little. We have to ride tomorrow. We need to keep your muscles from stiffening overmuch." They rose and walked slowly toward a scattering of grybins nibbling the late spring grass. Rataq limped along, tentatively reaching out and around with the arm that had hung limp yesterday.

"So far all you have said is 'disaster.' Tell me what actually happened."

Rataq sighed and began. "We could not return secretly to Colufo. Our captives would betray us. I do not kill in cold blood. So we flew to the caves where many 'O' and 'F' families fled when Eckem Meluq proved he had become a vicious dictator."

"I thought your Eckem was in the ship."

"Oh, he is. He acts through his agents—Barsorq, Ubek, others. He has spies everywhere, ears everywhere. He fears losing control, with the limits of living opening out to an entire planet instead of just within the skin of the ship. He knew and he waited. He is more malefic in his tyranny than even I had believed. In the middle of one night, one evil facinorous night, they arrested all the leaders of my organization, killed all the resisters and imprisoned the rest in the cells under Castle Colufo. One night destroyed my years of building. I had groups in each of the families. All gone in one night." He moaned the words. "Now I cannot fight. Now I can only run. I am nothing."

"You have a communicator."

Rataq's fingers fumbled for the red jewel on the chain around his neck. "Yes. It was Ubeq's. But there is no one. . . ." His gaze dropped back to his feet.

Brian switched to different ideas. "There is Kel-Ufar."

Rataq raised his head and smiled a weary smile. "Yes, Kel-Ufar. I *would* like to ride Kel-Ufar against the wind, under the arching sky."

Brian pointed. "There she is."

Lazo Rataq looked and called. Kel-Ufar raised her head from the grass. Her ears pointed toward Rataq, she whickered. She lifted her tail in an arch and trotted toward them. He arose, rubbed her sniffing nose, patted her neck and chest. "She remembers." He grinned.

"She is not zotoed."

Rataq squinted at Brian, eyes threatening. "Enough! You have belabored that idea enough."

Brian smiled. He had struck a spark.

## twelve

Rataq leaned against the soft warm flank of Kel-Ufar, fixed Brian with his eyes across her back. "There is Ngora. We were going after Ngora and Mirren. Give me a few days' rest, then let us do that. There is nothing else."

"Two of us against a tribe?"

"Why not? I have brought a blaster. With surprise we might give Xergin and Togrel and the rest a good battle."

"Surprise? Like the last time? But that's my Rataq. You are feeling better."

Rataq worked his shoulders. "I'm still sore, but this is something to do."

"They are on their way to the Dormala, the gathering. It would be hard to find them before they arrive. Inibek says we can fight for them at the Nyada battles." Inside, Brian cringed. He had brooded long sleepless nights and found no better way than Inibek's.

He returned to questions. "What happened at the caves? Will the people not support you?"

Rataq shook his head. "They are the 'O' and 'F' families, trained for generations not to lead, just to accept. They expended all their daring when they fled. It will take all their spirit to protect themselves in those caves."

"But if you make a first move won't they back you up?"

Rataq shook his head. "They would greatly prefer me to Meluq for eckem, but they will do nothing to bring it about. I left Ubeq a prisoner there. I am not even confident that they will keep him.

"After two days we started back, Girto and I. Only with integrity do I give my word to return. But as soon as we rose in the air, an air car was upon us. They had mounted a small paser gun in their ship. Its weight and the weight of its power source made them slow. Still, if we tried to use our speed to fly off, the ray would have burned us. We maneuvered, we dodged, twisted. Girto is a good pilot. But we could not evade that ray forever.

"We smashed into them and the crash destroyed their control, but we went down too. Girto fought the car down and landed without further damage. We spent days attempting repairs. The best we could do was to restore enough power to lift one of us. Girto went back to the caves. I flew this far, coming up the river, and now the car is at the highest altitude it can attain. It can go no higher."

"Can we use its comm gear?"

"Smashed."

Brian groaned.

Rataq still stood beside Kel-Ufar, running his hands over the short warm fur of her neck and shoulders. "We have to face the facts, Brian McCann. We are beaten. Let Eckem Meluq and Ubeq have their victory. Perhaps we can live for awhile among the nomads before they finally seek us out and slay us. Eventually it will happen, but we can live for today: ride our grybins, fight for our women, enjoy the wind and the sun a little while before we die."

Brian glared into Rataq's hopeless eyes. "You can quit. Your people have landed safely. Your children, your precious children, will grow to manhood. You lose only yourself. My people have not yet landed. They approach. You condemn them to death. I cannot quit."

"Ah, yes." Rataq's face was sad. "But what can you do?"

Brian considered. "Your Rogo and Woluf and your scouting ship must have made some surveys before they settled on Colufo as the site for building their land-launch tube."

"To a certain extent, yes."

"What did they report?"

"Just what are you trying to learn?"

"We agreed to settle our people in widely separated areas, to avoid conflict and to stop interfering with the Thana."

"What is the point? We are whipped."

"All that may be. Still, what did your surveys show?"

Rataq shrugged. "Great expanses of empty seas. Great expanses of empty lands. Only two, perhaps three, limited areas of civilization of a rather low order. We selected Colufo, home of the Thana, a nonaggressive population large enough to make a work force to help us establish our high order of organized society in comfort, without excessive stress."

"And Eckem Meluq will tyrannize over it."

Brian rested his hands on Kel-Ufar's back, face to face with Rataq. "Now I will tell you my projection. This land has the water and the green and a warm red sun. It has the wind that bends the grass and rosy clouds against a dark blue sky. A man can feel himself in this world." He bit off the next words sharply. "If he has worked for it. And you, Lazo Rataq, have worked for it. You have endured. You are in no way a quitter. Look at this land. Get your people out of the city, out of the caves. Let them work the land—our people, your people, yes, and the Thana too. We all have skills to teach and a need to learn."

"Leave Colufo?"

"Leave Colufo."

"Our work force?"

"Do your 'O' and 'F' families at the caves have any Thana slaving for them?"

"A few are showing them how to grow belele in the caves."

"Teachers, not slaves. You endured the tough physical life until you liked it. You enjoy the heat of the sun, the crisp cold of the night. You enjoy using those strong developing muscles, you enjoy learning and using new skills—a man among men, riding, herding, guiding and feeling the response of a good mount. You look forward to the transporting pleasure of riding a magnificent animal, this Kel-Ufar. You have done something hard to do: you have had the sweet delight of being alive in a bright, beautiful world, and it is all new, scarcely touched. Relish it.

"Now if you use Thana slaves for work, your Litani will never experience what you experienced. They will always be dissatisfied, want more sensory input, more amusement, more satisfaction. Idle hands and idle minds holding arbitrary power over others always want more power, scheme for it, fight for it, and always fear losing it. They become paranoid in their fears if their power is not always growing. Isn't this your Eckem Meluq? His hysterical fear of losing his power haunts his sleepless nights.

"Muscles grow strong only with use. Capability of the mind grows only with use. An organization grows strong by meeting challenge with response—

sucessful response, that is. A nation of people grows strong through struggle and action. A dream of peace when all struggle is over, and desires are granted with little effort, is a false dream. Such a peace leads to deterioration and disaster. Your people need to work to develop and build their own farms and communities. They need to feel the result of their own effort and their own skills. That makes unshakeable confidence. They then know that what they did once they can do again. No one can take that from them. End of lecture."

Rataq looked up and grinned wryly. "All those beautiful ideas after we have lost."

Children riders were racing toward them, threading through the grazing herd, rushing pell mell, playing a kind of tag. Ekai in the lead dodged around grybins, making sharp cuts, sticking to his saddle pad like he was glued. Alungo and Oarda followed, just as tight on their mounts, trying to get close enough to snatch the strip of fur that flopped about behind Ekai, held only by the pressure of elbow against his side. Shouts, laughing, excited faces.

Brian and Rataq smiled and waved as they tore on by. "Children, precious children, you said. Will those of your people ever be like that, running the wind?"

"Enough, enough, it is over."

"But it is not over. Your jewel now, your micheli. Can we raise the *Plymouth* with that?"

Rataq shook his head. "It has no power to reach out into space. It can go to Colufo, or perhaps even to the orbiting ship when it is directly overhead, but no further."

"Can we talk to Eckem Meluq?"

"It would just give him our location."

"Exactly."

"You want to have us killed sooner than. . . ."

He stopped suddenly. "It might give us a chance." He closed his eyes, thoughtful. Then he slapped Kel-Ufar on the rump. "We could try."

"Better than just waiting. The last time they found us you gained an air car and a blaster."

"Next time perhaps they will burn us down from the air."

"Maybe."

Rataq was fingering his jewel setting.

"Can you raise your ship right now?"

"Every night, nearly every night, I have been on Vassa, I have watched for it. I know its orbit and its period. Yes, I believe it will be in range." Rataq held up his jewel in his hand.

"You don't call?"

"The carrier triggers reception. Each micheli has its own frequency. He will think it is Ubeq."

A moment of waiting, then, with a crackling background, came words in Eckem Meluq's authoritative growl. "Terko! Where are ... Lazo Rataq! About time you showed up." The voice curled into suave solicitude. "You look worn out and beaten up. You must be tired of running with the crude and filthy natives. Ready to come in?"

Rataq held his micheli away from his face, winked and grinned at Brian. Then he spoke softly to his jewel. "Look, Eckem, swar, I have very little time. Soon we will be riding with the natives. I just wanted to tell you," his voice turned harsh, "if you really want me, why do you not come down and find me yourself? You old flatulent, odoriferous, grotesquely obese tyrant!" He spoke the last words slowly and with great precision, then shut off transmission and let the micheli swing on its chain.

"Was that long enough for a fix?" Brian asked.

"Of a certainty. His computer has our coordinates to a few meters. He will be after us as soon as his air cars are assembled and airborne. We must be watchful. I will keep my blaster ready."

## thirteen

Eckem Meluq's massive body sat immobile as a fat rock. He could not believe the words that still pounded in his ears. In a state of shock his breathing ceased. His flushed face slowly turned blue.

Suddenly he gasped for air and yelled at the intercom, "Uruq ligif, when will those air cars be ready?"

Over the speaker, Uruq answered. "Two weeks more, Eckem, swar. There is much to be done."

"Get with it, or I'll have your eyeballs!" He sat boiling in his command chair, mumbling to himself, "Why would Rataq talk to me... me!... like that? He knows I won't come myself. Can't stand that gravity. But why?"

He beat his pudgy hands together. "I know what it is," he said aloud. "He thinks he can capture an air car again. Well, I'll send one he won't capture, and an army with it."

He leaned forward to call Barsorq.

In the Kiyatagu camp the early morning bustled with the stowing of dismantled torkas on wagons, household goods on tipulas, and the forming up the herds for the trek.

Brian watched the loading of one slab-sided tipula kneeling with short thick legs tucked under; its face was disdainful, lower jaw chewing in a loose rotary motion, long lashes on drooping eyelids. It seemed oblivious to everything but the enjoyment of its cud. From time to time it hooked, half heartedly, toward the kovas swarming around with their loading, but from long experience they were wary. From a wooden frame on the tipula's back they hung red leather bags of the dried meat and curds. They piled felt mats on top and a woman with a babe settled herself in a hollow. She jerked the single rein pegged into the tipula's nose. The animal grunted, groaned, stretched out its long neck like a thick, hairy snake, and swung its head from side to side in a slow, regal motion. Then it began to rise, hind legs first that tossed the woman forward, front legs up that tossed her back again. But she remained calm, unconcerned, suckling the babe at her breast the whole time.

The march was organized very much the way the Sukota had done it, spreading out across the valley. Except now Brian and Rataq—leading his Kel-Ufar—rode on grybin back. Before long their rising way narrowed into a pass between low mountains. Herds pressed together, and there was no grazing along the way. Still, the grade was easy. The wagons had no difficulties.

Unshod hooves struck a muffled clatter on a hard surface. Could that surface be a pavement? Brian watched it closely as he rode. Most of it was hard-trodden dirt, but occasionally a bare smooth surface extended for many meters. Cracked uneven edges showed. More and more Brian believed they followed an ancient roadway. He kicked his mount into a trot to pull up beside Inibek.

"Is this an old road with its pavement?"

"What is pavement?"

Brian thought, of course he has no experience with pavement. "A special hard surface put down so wheels roll easily."

"Ah, yes, hard smooth surface." Inibek nodded. "There are places."

"And a roadway made so it is not too steep anywhere, hills cut down, ravines filled in or bridged?"

Inibek thought for a moment. "Yes, even in the mountains there are easy ways for wagons. Nalpur of Runn declared it should be that way and it was that way, so the tribes could travel to the Dormala, to come together to pay tribute to Nalpur of Runn."

"What is this tribute?"

"When a god makes the way easy for you, when he brings the fire down for you to use, when he puts the stars and the moons and the yann in the sky to make light for you and warmth in the day, it is well to pay one's respects, to lay one's shamshuls in the sacred caves, to give thanks for the light and the fire, for the grass and the trees, for the herds, all the animals." He gestured, both arms outspread, and shot a glance at Brian. "You are a messenger of the god Llu, worshipped by the Thana in the lowlands. How does your Llu act if no one bows down? Does he not send miseries? Does he not send tempests? Does he not send plague among the people who express no faith in him?"

Brian merely nodded. He did not want to answer that one. He had claimed to be a messenger only to stop the Thana from calling him a god. That path always led to awkward positions.

On their third night, relaxed after a meal of magli jerky and raw loggets, Inibek, Kors, Brian and Rataq sat by their small fire, robes pulled snug against the chill air. Inibek rested his back along the warm side of Kel-Biret. So also did Rataq with Kel-Ufar. As yet he had not ridden, but now, with his good rapport, Inibek said tomorrow he would ride.

On the road, for the most part Rataq had been silent, fondling his Kel-Ufar at every pause in the march, his whole attention on her and his private thoughts, except that, with his hand on the blaster at his belt, he looked often at the sky.

Inibek Kob chewed leaves of the saad. Now that life had returned to a routine, even without Benjak and Oveda, perhaps even more because he lived without Benjak and Oveda, he allowed himself the indulgence of the saad and the relaxing dreams it brought.

"Tell us more of Nalpur and the ceremonies of the gathering," Brian asked.

"Ah, yes, the Dormala, Nalpur, the great warrior, the great herdsman. The things he taught us." He paused to spit. "In the olden times we made do on the roots we could find and dig, and the gonfis we killed throwing rocks. There is little meat on a gonfi's bones, and that little is not tasty like the magli." He sucked his teeth, exploring for a remaining bit of meat.

"And there are the words of the beginning. There was a Vassa before the beginning; the words say that. I have not understood that. There are many of the sacred words that are difficult to understand." He chewed slowly on his leaves of saad, then shifted the wad to his cheek and spoke again. "In the beginning was the cloud of fire. Vassa came out of the cloud of fire. Then out of the sacred mountain, Runn, great fire throne mountain, out of the sacred caves there, came Nalpur of Runn. There is yet fire from fire throne mountain—a quiet fire. You will see. When there are no clouds, sometimes even yet it burns from afar. When you saw the gleam, was it not strong and bright? One sees it, the fire from the mountaintop, from many places, at many times, far from the mountain. Sometimes it changes colors. Sometimes it burns the eyes."

Brian puzzled again. It was a strange kind of a light.

One of Kob's women came to add dung bricks to the dying fire.

Brian asked, "Can one climb the mountain to see the source of the light?"

Inibek shook his head. "It is the sacred mountain. No one climbs Altar Durno Runn."

Brian held the thought that he would find a way to investigate the red light that sometimes changed its color. He went on to other questions. "You have not told us what actually goes on at the gathering."

"Yes, it is time to speak of the Dormala." Inibek stretched his legs to a more comfortable position. "At the Dormala we do many things. But all is in praise of Nalpur of Runn. We see old friends."

"Old friends? I thought you were warring tribes."

"There are raids. There are battles. But on the other hand we are one people, the Thana-Kovas, so there are friends also. Sisters who married out of the tribe meet with brothers. Fathers see daughters this once a year." He shrugged. "There is trading. Some Kovas make better bows. Some make better arrowheads. There is racing of grybins. Often there is dancing through the night—dances praising Nalpur and remembering a great battle or a great hunt."

"You spoke of fighting for women as if it were like a duel."

"The Nyada battles—they are an important happening that lasts four days. Each day all the girls from one tribe who have seen sixteen gatherings are staked out in a line about twenty meters apart. In times long ago an ankle was tied by a thong to the stake, but we found no binding was needed. They enjoy it. Nothing like having several Kovas fighting for possession to make a girl feel the strength of her powers." He laughed. "Anyway, if they run they would be disgraced, outcasts losing themselves in the mountains. Rarely has this happened."

"Then the battles?"

"Not yet the battles. First the Kovas stroll back and forth on the field looking over the girls, studying the men who will fight. Most know the girl and have a good guess who they will have to fight. Still, they take that last look over the choices. It is good not to let the girls be too sure of one's interest. Later on one has the task of teaching the woman her place." He chewed reflectively on his saad. "That too can be interesting.

"When yann is highest the battles begin, first companions together against others." The light in his eyes quickened with memories. "Some girls attract several pairs of companions. It is no disgrace at this time, before they draw and clash their blades, for men who are not great warriors to withdraw or to seek a second choice, or a third. That is good judgment. After they begin, a man who fights well but is bested, wounded so he cannot continue, is still respected. But a man who runs away before the fight is decided loses his honor. When Benjak and I fought for Oveda...."

"I thought you captured her in a raid."

"Yes, that is so. Still, at the first gathering after a capture, if someone calls for her, the woman is staked out with the others. Against Benjak and me there were Pukar and Esend. They were foolish, but they were brave. Benjak killed Esend, felled him with one mighty cut, took off one leg at the hip and cut nearly through the other above the knee. He died quickly in a rush of blood. Pukar threw down his sword. That is surrender when it is two against one. I could have killed him, but I did not, that time. I should have, but he had been brave."

In his command chair, Eckem Meluq rocked from side to side on his hams. These days his buttocks were beginning to ache from supporting much weight with little relieving movement. His eyes devoured the lands and the seas of Vassa spread before him on his comm screen.

It was his planet. He had brought all his people back to their own. Now they were planeted while he still orbited. He gripped the arms of his chair until knuckles showed through the flesh. "It's my planet."

In deep space he had taken command when tensions were building toward a great explosion, families were arming for a showdown. Blaster-rayed death was imminent for many. Personally he had disarmed the leaders of the F and O families—he was young then, strong and quick—and personally he forced return to the old ways that had kept peace on the ship through generations of travel around the curve of space, re-establishing the absolute dominance of the Q family. You can't carry passengers with no duties on a trip that lasts for centuries. Duties had to be assigned—and carried out.

And even before that, he was the one who interpreted the age-old records accurately. He made the plan, enforced the plan, and brought the ship home. His planet, but it was too much even to climb to the vitriport for a direct look. He sighed and slumped in his seat, then thumbwheeled the comm screen to its finest resolution. The planet zoomed toward him until he could see moving figures in the crooked jumble of streets that was Colufo. He strained to recognize figures, he fiddled with switches. The figures still were tiny dots. He could not distinguish Litanofoq from Thana.

A light flashed on the control board. Meluq switched to communications. Barsorq's face appeared.

"Where were you last report time?" Meluq growled.

"Busy prodding that Thana army along. They are now well on their way toward the mountain valley where the nomads have retreated. The passes are not guarded. They expect nothing. We are air lifting our Q forces up to them close to the final pass as fast as the air cars can get them there. Enough Thana leaders are zotoes. They will fight."

"You are sending no Os and Fs?"

"They went to the caves."

"Yes, I know. But have you no Q commanders there?"

"I sent commanders and masters. They were refused entry."

"By Golak, your commanders are incompetent! The Os and Fs are out of control. Do I have to come down there and show you how. . . ." A red warning light flashed.

Eckem Meluq pressed the annunciator switch. A radar display replaced Barsorq's face. The center of the display was Meluq's ship, bright range rings marked dark space outward in 100,000-sora increments. At the far edge a tiny arrow pointed to a blip, a moving newcomer, a bogie. Meluq punched questions into his EDP unit. Distance, dimensions, rates of approach. He grunted and switched back to Barsorq. "Ship nearing. If it does not alter speed, it will reach my orbit in three or four Vassa days. Get the battle over with. Get ready to talk scout ships, shuttles, whatever, into crash range of Colufo. We will crash each ship that comes close. Then we will mount our heaviest paser ray gun in a shuttle. Their ship is unarmed."

He thumbed the comm screen toward Kovas territory to see if he could locate his army.

## fourteen

They traveled a leisurely two weeks, pushing the herds a few soras each day, grazing slowly up a narrow valley, then shoving hard for two days over a high pass into another valley. Always there were higher and higher mountains before them. The days on the road healed Lazo Rataq's body, gave him clear eyes and wiry muscles. He rode Kel-Ufar with confidence and a grim zest. And he and Brian watched the sky.

During the trek Brian reverted to the almost forgotten Earthside occupation of anthropology. He talked often with Inibek around the evening fire, and during the day he sought out Inibek's sons and daughter. He learned that the Thana-Kovas were patrilineal, and that made tracing lineage a bit complicated, with two lines of fathers. Yet the boys knew their begats completely back through at least six generations: 128 paternal grandfathers. They knew their uncles—their fathers' brothers, that is—and their uncles' uncles and all the begatted cousins from all the uncles. Some chart, thought Brian. Oarda knew two generations, all that was required of girls; but, along with Ekai and Alungo, she knew of the beginnings of all the tribes.

When the brothers—Kiyatagu, the eldest, and Juro, Sokota and Buka—found Nalpur of Runn after he had been driven from the sacred mountain, they carried him to their torka where their sister nursed his burns. He had captured fire, but it rebelled. It broke out to throw Nalpur out of the mountain of Runn. He was a god, so as soon as he was well again he went back into the mountain. There he caught the fire again and tamed it to do his will. But he was lonely. The god, who had never known a woman before, had known Tendra, the sister of the four brothers. So again he came down out of the mountain, this time in search of Tendra.

In that time the brothers and their wives wandered widely, finding the wild grain where it grew and digging the roots suitable for eating where they grew, yet in those days there was no light and the things that came from the ground did not know how to grow well.

Nalpur in his search carried no water, and Kiyatagu found him in a desert, withered and staggering from thirst. Again the brothers succored him, and they gave him Tendra to wife. He lived with them for many years and, living with them, he learned what their needs were. So he threw the fire that was yann, the sun, up into the sky for light in the day to make the plants grow better, and he made the rain fall and the rivers run. He gave each of the brothers a pair of koana, tagu and mesor, and he saw that they multiplied. He also gave them magli and tipula, and they also multiplied. Seeing that they needed a riding animal to herd the koana and the magli, he gave them grybins. Then finally he went back into the fire throne mountain, taking Tendra with him.

Now the clans of each brother multiplied, and with their great herds finding enough grass was difficult. So they separated and went their ways apart.

At last the trek reached Gompani, the mountain-girt valley of the Dormala. A wide lush valley it was, green with many grasses, well watered, with running streams joining into a small river that meandered across midvalley to disappear down a cleft between snowcapped peaks.

On Kel-Birat Inibek straightened up from his riding slouch to gaze at the panorama. "Grass for many dhols," he said, "even for all the herds. Nalpur always greens our valley."

Brian followed his gaze toward Altar Durno Runn, great fire throne mountain, a blocky crag with swirling dark strata spiraling upward higher and higher like black tongues of flame solidified, but still straining toward the sky.

It was not the highest mountain. Others taller, more massive, jutted up into the muddy pink clouds, where shreds streamed away on the tearing wind with remnants only pinned by sharp peaks against the blue sky. But Brian understood at once that fire throne mountain would be the one to gather legends. Even without the fire, it was the mountain of character. And just what was that fire? He could see no sign of it now.

"Look at the hills across the valley," Inibek said.

Brian searched those hills with his eyes. "Dark glossy splotches. Fused rock?"

"They are from Nalpur's time when much fire burst from the mountain. Even today beams reach out high up. You have seen them from afar. Nalpur protects the valley, but sometimes still he burns those hills."

Beside them, Rataq on Kel-Ufar studied the swirling mountain. Quietly he said, "I have seen that mountain before."

Inibek looked puzzled. Brian looked his question.

"On our micro-reader of Litanofoq and Vassa

history. It was long ago, and I did not know at the time that it was important. I cannot remember the details. Perhaps a closer look...."

When Brian descended to the valley floor, Kors and Cogbard were there before him.

Cogbard met Brian with a puzzled yet contrite look on his wide black face. "Some great thing in my head kept screaming, "Kill! Kill! It kept saying it for many dhols after we left the camp. It must be that the devil god Gerzu has entered me." He knelt on both knees, bowed his head, and touched Brian's scabbard with his fingers. "Vanth Nugol is a great sword, a biting blade washed in the blood of battle. Make a clean stroke. Do it quickly."

Brian looked at Kors, who shook his head sadly. "He has begged death of me ever since the screaming faded away."

Brian drew his sword briskly. He laid it against Cogbard's neck—gently. "Vanth Nugol refuses to slice," he said solemnly, and sheathed his sword again.

"I am your slave." Cogbard bowed to the ground.

"You are a great warrior. Rise to be like one. We may have need."

Cogbard remained on his knees. "There is something else. Before, I could not speak of it, my mind stopped moving whenever the thought came into it. Only now can I speak." He turned his head to look at Kors. "This I heard at Tsankta. The Litani do not know I was listening. They said they were gathering an army to send after you. And the Old Litani have far-kill weapons."

A Thana army! Brian had helped arm and train that army, fought with them to overthrow the Vanth. Now a Thana army pursuing him.... They were thorough, those Litani; if Cogbard did not get him the army would. But a battle between Thana and Thana-Kovas, and because of him! A cold shiver slid down his spine, hard and cutting as a spear point. With a mechanical wave of his hand he wheeled and strode off in search of Rataq. He found him lounging on a grassy knoll watching the grazing Kel-Ufar.

"Rataq, Cogbard says Barsorq is sending a Thana army to find us. Would he do that?"

Looking up with quick comprehension in his eyes, Rataq said, "Of course, that is what is happening. That's why there is no air car. It will be an army and the car together. Of course. They will use zotoed Thanas, backed by a few Litani, with an air car directing from above, shooting down. Eckem Meluq is making this what you call a big time affair."

Brian groaned. "It's a fight, then, between Thana and Kovas. I can't have them fighting each other just to get me. And you too." He stared off across the valley, thinking aloud. "Could we stop it, I wonder—give ourselves up, maybe?" He pulled at his red beard.

Rataq looked up at Brian, eyes wide. "Ridiculous. How will that help your *Plymouth*? Nor will I surrender myself. That won't slow them, anyway. They will go on to capture Ngora and Lieutenant Fitzgerald. Also the Kovas are great warriors. They will make a tough battle. It may not be so easy to capture us."

"You are right, of course." Brian beat one fist into his other hand. "We taunted Meluq into it. What we have to do now is find a way to use his anger before too much good blood stains the grass. Mirren and Ngora will be in the valley by now. We must find them."

"First we must warn Inibek."

Inibek's teeth showed white in laughter. "Thana attack us! Ho, ho! Never. Never till the yann turns dark and falls from the sky. Ha. . . ."

Brian cut into his scoffing. "Not the usual Thana, but Thana driven on by Litani."

Cogbard straightened his massive shoulders. He seemed to grow taller, and menacing. His hand darted to his sword hilt. He glared eye to eye with Inibek. He was just as large, just as heavily muscled. "I am Thana!" he spit out. "We whipped the Vanth." Then he slumped. "But this should not be. It is as he says, the Thana are being forced by Litani. And they have far-kill weapons."

Still grinning, Inibek answered, "Even with these old Litani, the Thana will never face Kovas in battle."

Rataq and Kors held their words, but their faces were grim.

But to satisfy his friends, companions who suffered captivity by his side and who were together with him in their escape, Inibek agreed to set a lookout at the pass.

That was next to nothing, Brian thought. He felt pounded flat and left to dry in the sun, like the jerky the women prepared for the trek. He sighed and asked, "What will the Sukota do if I go to their camp looking for Mirren?"

"Nothing at all, unless you try to bring her away. In the morning I go to a meeting of deitches at the camp of the Buka. The Sukota camp is on the way. I will show you."

Rataq spoke. "What will happen if I ride Kel-Ufar there?"

Inibek Kob grinned. "Nothing, nothing at all but daggering looks. In the valley there is no fighting except for the Nyada."

Except when the Thana arrive, Brian thought.

Their way led past the mountain of Runn. As they neared, Brian gazed at the black strata twisting skyward, and slightly above the valley floor he could see the forbidding dark mouth of the caves. The low symmetrical arch seemed manmade. Rataq swung toward it for a closer look. There was a huge slanting ramp of black rock with steps cut reaching to the archway. Manmade surely, Brian thought. By the Old Litani, melted out with their heat laser.

When they dismounted, Kob looped together the reins of Kel-Birat, Kel-Ufar and Brian's mount. "The Kel-grybins will stand," he said. "Go not beyond the entryway. The caves are holy. Also danger lies deep in the mountain."

Brian peered in from the mouth. A faint fetid smell drifted on stale air. Across the dim vaulted space he saw three black openings. To his right and left against the walls, small dark objects were piled.

"Shumshuls of the ashes of our revered ones," Inibek said.

"So many?"

"And more in the rooms beyond." Their voices bounced in hollow echoing.

The floor and the walls, as high as Brian could see into the shadow, were glassy black, the solidification of melted rock, very similar to the secret ways under Colufo. But this was the work of the Old Litani, centuries ago. There was a core of truth in the myths of Nalpur of Runn. Brian felt drawn toward those dark openings, a fascination pulling but also a fear repelling. Was Nalpur of the Old Litani a scientist perhaps, protected from the holocaust inside the mountain? Maybe there were several of them. Brian looked toward Rataq. He was examining colored patterns on the wall.

"What is the danger deep inside?" Rataq asked.

"Grutmaul and Grutmaul's children lie in wait in the dark and the damp. It is a brave man with great love for his father who places his shumshul in the holiest place far inside. Those who are not very brave or who do not care very much, scurry in here, drop their shumshuls and scuttle out again like gonfis. Grutmaul and her little ones are stirring now. They know that the time for hunting is near. On the day of the Tsuring after the Nyada battles is the time men carry shumshuls into the caves. Now we go on to my meeting."

Rataq was silent and thoughtful as they rode on.

Side by side stood the three of them, Mirren, Ngora and Oveda, each with her tall leather bag and long paddle, stirring kukri. There was need for much kukri in the evenings at the Dormala. As Brian approached his eyes clung to Mirren, her golden hair sun bleached nearly white in startling contrast to her weatherbeaten face. Her aristocratic nose was red and peeling. Her eyes were the same color blue as they had been, but the muscles around them had taken on a squint against the sun and wind. Her tattered uniform was pinned together with long desert thorns. How would she receive him?

His eyes dropped to the kukri bag, bulging, folding, wrinkling as Mirren stirred. His stomach felt like that, rolling and gripping with tension. He sucked a long breath against the lurching. It was guilt. He had escaped and had left her a slave—the fair Irish maiden who was also the sophisticated captain of a space ship. And his news had to be, no rescue, just a duel still some days away and the threat of an approaching Thana army.

Body straight, expression masked, she watched his step slow as he neared. He hesitated, trying to find the right words. She had been through an ordeal, and he had done nothing, just waited. He needed to show sympathy, to explain. He wanted to know what had happened and yet he really did not want to hear what he greatly feared might have happened. How to begin?

He stuttered, "How, how are you, Mirren? How have you been?"

She continued stirring. "Just fine."

"That is good. You look well."

"How has it been with you?"

"Oh, I'm fine. Have they treated you well?"

"Oh, very well, considering."

"Considering what?"

"Considering how long we have been alone with them."

Brian's gut twisted like an auger bit. He burst out, "Mirren, for God's sake!" His voice came out a raspy squawk. "What did they do to you?"

Mirren glanced at Ngora, talking with Rataq, at Inibek who, after speaking a few words with Oveda, was riding away to his meeting. "Well," she said slowly, still stirring in the leather bag, "They fed us, gave us a place to sleep, and worked us like slaves. I am tough as spring steel."

"Damn it, Mirren! You are infuriating. Among these barbarous nomads, the men with all their wives and their concubines...." He broke off, aware of the dignified figure of Oveda. Her steady gaze pierced him through and through. He laid his hand to his sword hilt, then dropped it again.

Mirren chuckled. "Oh, that. We are protected prizes to be fought over at the Nyada battles. We have many suitors. Will you be there?"

Brian's face flamed red. "Blast! You are laughing at me." He sucked a deep breath, looked around to see Ngora grinning. Suddenly he grinned too, feeling tension flow away. "Serve you right if I stay clear of those battles. But I'll be there. I'll take you away. You can be my slave, you can wait on me, gather dung for my fires."

Mirren held out both hands. "Peace," she said.

"Peace, it has been a long time."

Brian took her in his arms. After long moments he remembered and held her away from him. "I have to tell you the bad news. We believe the Litani have gathered an army of Thana—controlled, of course—and all just to capture us."

Mirren gasped. "Our Thana friends fighting Kovas—that's bitter. And the *Plymouth* must be nearing by now." They stood together, arms, hands touching, each in his or her own thoughts searching for an answer, minds buzzing as futile as flies at a windowpane.

"Is there nothing we can do?"

"There has to be something. We need communication. Rataq's micheli is too short range. But if we can capture an air car . . . we did once. We might fly to Colufo and last long enough to send out a warning. We might ride to meet that army and suprise them somehow. But our chances will be better in the confusion of the battle. . . ."

"We can't leave. We are watched at all times."

Now Brian heard little shuffling noises behind him. He swung around to see a ring of silent Sukota surrounding them, where before there had been only casual tribesmen doing camp chores.

## fifteen

In the daytime there were races, Kel-grybins flying along a marked track in the fields. There were contests demonstrating skills with the lance and with bows, all while pounding by on grybin back. In the evening around campfires the tribes relaxed to the euphoria of the chewing of saad, told tales, sang songs, and there was dancing through the night.

The Kovas danced as if they were still on their mounts, knees bent to a half-sitting crouch, bodies bobbing, ducking, swaying, to grybin rhythms, trotting, running, charging down on enemies, pursuing chladni in a joyous hunt, warily circling klugons in a hazardous hunt. The young men rotated, wheeled, spun about the fire twirling, gyrating, reeling, each acting his own story in dance, all moving to the beat of the small drums, the saddle drums used in war to direct maneuvers. Feet shuffled, stamping in the dust, voices shouted wordless sounds, crying out in the hot excitement of battle.

The great circle wound around, a Kovas darting out, arm whipping a spear, then dropping back among the mass of dancers. A twisting body stretched his bowstring, launching arrows. Another man rode in the midst of enemies, whirling his sword in great arcs, cutting down the foes. Savages in the flickering firelight, joyous faces seized by memories and dreams of combat, living them again in the dance.

And around them in a still greater circle stood the girls, solemn faced, quietly watching. They thought it was all a show for them. Who were the great hunters? Who were the great providers, the great warriors, the great protectors? It was all for them, the races, the riding contests, the contests with weapons. Solemn faced they gazed, smiling inwardly as they watched all the fine young men. And when the girls knew, when they decided, they let the men know, with eyes, with perky ears, with arched necks and over-the-shoulder glances. All the maneuvering to bring chosen triples together would save many strong lives on Nyada battle days. When it was clear that a maiden favored only one pair of companions and they favored her, the battle might be a demonstration only. But the girls who vacillated, or those who clutched their pride around them and sent their glances toying with several pairs from different tribes, would see a bloody battle.

The men too had their selections. Some would not heed the messages, and that led to battles. All kinds arranged themselves for the Nyada dhols, the days of the marriage battles—four days, one for the girls of each tribe.

Early in the morning of the fourth day of the Nyada battles, after Inibek Kob had ridden off to reclaim Oveda with the cutting edge of his sword, Ekai and Alungo left quietly on another mission. They were still too young to attend the Nyada. Slipping along behind them, taking care not to be seen, Oarda followed. She had noticed them take up their shumshuls. She knew what that meant, and she greatly feared what they were going to do. But a small sister could not stop two big brothers from walking into danger.

In the entry room of the caves, standing close together, Ekai and Alungo hesitated. The only light coming from the arched entrance behind them seemed to soak up and disappear into the dead black walls. Ekai struck flint to tinder, flamed his torch into the cold silence.

From outside, Oarda called in desperate dread.

Alungo answered, "Go along, little sister, you can't come in here. We are going to carry ours." With his toe he nudged a tablet at the base of a pile. "We will lay ours in a place of honor, even in the room of thrones where Nalpur of Runn reigns over all the lesser ones. Father Benjak will be among the best of the gods. Father Inibek will be proud. But don't you tell him until we return." His voice trembled a bit toward the last words.

He raised his dagger-sized sword, held it ready before him and stepped toward the dark opening in the center wall. Ekai followed with his torch into the chill of the black corridor. Both ignored the colored lines on the wall that reached upward into the dimness of the vaulted space above.

Each boy held his shumshul against his chest. Alungo had the low relief in clay and ashes of Father Benjak on Kel-Nirza wreathed in flames, formed as well as his hands could make it, and his hands had modeled with skill. His throat felt chokey. He pressed forward, flicking his sword at the dark. This was to tell the tribe he was a worthy son of Benjak and Inibek. At nine years he could do a man's deed.

Ekai, a head taller, stalked behind, his thought spiked on thorns of worry, thinking on how to keep Alungo from going farther than was safe. He remembered Father Benjak lying in the spring sun; he had refused to stay in the torka, demanded to feel the warm red rays of the yann and to let the wind carry away the stink of the black rotting flesh with greenish tints that grew along his thigh. Benjak put the responsibility on Ekai. "Alungo has the drive to do without thought. He is like a young magli, capering about, dashing away from the herd with no thought that a hunting klugon may be hiding in the grass. You must now be the man. Until Inibek returns, lead the clan and keep Alungo safe."

At the first side opening Ekai spoke. "We are well beyond the entry. In here we can leave our shumshuls. No one will call us cowards. There are many in this space." He held his torch high at the opening. "See how many are here." He pointed to dimly seen piles of votive tables.

"Would Father Inibek leave them here?" There was sharp scorn in Alungo's voice.

"You are not Inibek."

"Or would Benjak leave them here?"

"You are not Benjak."

"Neither will I. I am their son." He glanced at Ekai. "So are you. How can you think of stopping here?"

"I am their son also, and I have learned not to watch a campfire in a grass coat." He gazed into the black. "But better the spear in your breast than in your back," he muttered. Then, "I will go first," he said.

"So?" Alungo responded, and trotted ahead, the skin of his feet slapping on the slick black floor.

"Slowly, carefully," Ekai called, following quickly.

Alungo marched down a straight passageway with openings at regular intervals on each side. Frequently jagged fissures cleft the walls and overhead. Twice they stepped over cracks that split wide across the floor. It was through these cracks that the grutmauls came into the caves. Tales of encounters flooded Ekai's mind. The hair on the back of his neck rose up.

There was the great mother of grutmauls, it spread along a rock wall larger than a man, and there were her children, many smaller ones of many sizes. They were all arms that thickened in the middle where they came together. That was all there was to them, thick middle and arms reaching out, with some sort of an eye at the end of each arm. They had little hooking feet and also little suction cups along the arms. They could lie flat on a wall or a ceiling, creep along to drop down on a victim. When you tried to pull one off, stinging spines on the backs of their arms made you let go. There was no mouth or teeth, just an opening in the under side, and no need for it to get its food into that opening. It shoved its stomach outside, where it spread around on you, and acids oozed out of it to dissolve your flesh. The stomach absorbed it right there.

Ekai shuddered. He held his torch high into the next side opening. "There are only five shumshuls here. Only five in all of time have come this far. We are the sixth and seventh to dare this far. Let us leave them here."

"I will go until there are none. I will go farther than anyone." Alungo would not yield the lead.

Ekai held himself from yanking him back. A scuffle, with all their attention on each other.... No, he must watch every inch of the way, every crack, especially those in the ceiling. Light from his torch flared and dimmed, always changing, the shadows never still. Ekai strained his eyes ahead. Every moving shadow could be the tip of a grutmaul arm, ready to drop down on them.

They moved slowly now. Alungo also peered anxiously at the fluttering shadows. Still, step by step they pressed on, past a doorway where the gleam of light showed two tablets, past a door where the torch showed none at all, but Alungo insisted on going a little farther to be sure someone else had not skipped ahead. And somewhere there must be a great room of thrones.

Now unbidden their bodies moved closer. Their hands met and seemed of themselves to want to clasp but could not because each held something it could not drop. Ekai clutched his shumshul in that hand and Alungo gripped his small sword. As they came to each fissure overhead, he held the sword high toward the crack he could not reach, ready to stab at any dropping grutmaul.

There was cold silence except for the small crackle and hiss from the torch. There was dead black beyond the flickering splash of light close around them, moving as they moved. Shoulders touching, they crept onward in the center of the passage, more than an arm's length from each side. The acrid tang hanging in the still air had grown progressively stronger as they advanced into the mountain.

Ekai felt the presence of grutmauls in the dark before him, always in the black. When the light arrived there was nothing—until finally he saw a narrow shape, an arm hanging down from a crack in the ceiling, a whitish, colorless arm reaching toward them, an arm that sensed light.

"Quickly, Ekai. We'll get past."

They ran.

Ekai halted at the next opening. "Here. We are far beyond everybody. Father Inibek will be proud."

This time Alungo agreed. They turned in and immediately found themselves among many strange metallic blocky objects reaching just above their heads, a forest of them with narrow lanes between. They stretched row after row as far as they could see.

"The room of thrones!" Alungo whispered. He reached up to lay his shumshul on top of the nearest one. Ekai laid his beside it. Then back they started through the black hallway.

"Quickly now," Ekai said. "And watch for the cracks in the floor."

They ran, Alungo in front, Ekai behind, torch flaring with the motion. In time they saw the first wide gap in the floor, slowed to measure and jump. Before Ekai's gaze a grayish colorless mass dropped onto Alungo's head. His highpitched shriek echoed down the hallway.

Alungo dropped his blade, tore at the arm that reached down over his face. Ekai thrust the fiery torch at the writhing arms of the mass. Then with his free hand he grabbed an arm and jerked. He fought the pain like a hundred insect stings in his hand. It was a small grutmaul. It came free. He shook it from his hand into the fissure.

"Jump! Jump!"

Alungo leaped, then stumbled and fell on the other side.

Ekai gathered himself for the jump. A grutmaul plopped onto his shoulder, burned on his shoulder, sucking arms grasped around his neck. He was in the air crossing the gap. He dropped his torch, tore with both hands at slimey stinging arms on his chest. Alungo still lay on the floor, with two grutmauls on his back. He rolled and twisted to reach.

The torch sputtered on the floor beside him.

## sixteen

Mirren was up to see the red sun rise on the fourth day of the Nyada. Brian was a fine swordsman with his Vanth Nugol. He would have the reach. He towered over all but a few of the Thana-Kovas, but it would be two or more against him. She had a strong feeling of foreboding; unexpected things could happen. In the first three days of the Nyada she had seen savage fights to the death. She had seen melees where several Kovas attacked one pair, destroyed them and turned on each other. There seemed to be no rules except slash and stab. Defensively they used only a shield. They wore no armor. Many patches of grass lay trampled down soaked with Kovas blood.

Ngora stepped out of the torka beside Mirren, stretching the sleep from her body. Her gold tooth gleamed in a great yawn.

"You slept like a saad-drugged ox," Mirren complained.

Ngora's mouth snapped shut. "What's with you? Of course, Nyada."

"They make me feel like a subhuman slave. A Thana army is on the way. Our Sukota captors and our Kiyatagu friends will be fighting side by side against our Thana friends. What a mess!"

"You have to learn to roll with the punches, honey."

"And we are utterly helpless, utterly. It was almost better living day to day, knowing nothing, just a prisoner."

"Wearing half a tree trunk for a collar? Come off it, Mirren. And don't worry about Brian. He'll come through." She patted Mirren on the shoulder.

"At least as prisoners they left us alone."

Ngora grinned. "They saved us for today."

"Sex slaves for the animals to fight over."

"Early stage of civilization. Brawn is more decisive than brain. If you can remember, there are places on Earth where sheer power is still king of the hill."

"Ngora, how can you be so objective? You are in this right beside me. What about Rataq?"

Ngora's face froze. "That's why I work at being objective."

Mirren nodded sadly. "He hasn't much chance against these savages. They fight in pairs, companions." She paused. "And we came to these grasslands to find a refuge."

Ngora's face was somber. "I begged him to stay away. When we are delivered from this prisoner status, I ought to be able to bang the heads of any two furry husbands together. I'll get by."

Midway of the valley the line of stakes extended across from the looming rock swirls of great fire throne mountain, roughly parallel to the meandering river in the center. Thirty meters apart they marched, the sturdy posts set in years gone by when binding was felt to be needed. A short way up the valley were the piles of firewood, intermingled with herbal foliage, already gathered for the grand celebration for the dead. These were tengri herbs to bring loving happy memories of all who had passed on to live with Nalper, all the deitches and tribesmen. The Nyada in the afternoon, the marriages that evening, and the next evening celebration of the memories of the dead—these were the triple climaxes of the Dormala.

By late morning the Kovas were coming from all directions, beginning to form wide circles around the posts where they expected the battles to be the most thrilling.

Mirren stood rigid, one shoulder against her post, clinging to her dignity. Her once-white uniform was grayed with dirt ground into and unified with the fabric. Still, it was as clean as washing in the stream could make it. She had brushed the tangles from her golden hair with a Kovas brush. The red of her narrow aristocratic nose, that never quite turned brown like the rest of her face, she could do nothing about.

If the Kovas were going to fight over her she had to make some demonstration toward looking like a worthwhile prize, even if the whole affair was silly. Or would be silly if it were not so frustratingly serious. Her worried blue eyes gazed out over the gathering crowd toward the overcast sky. In her mind she saw the *Plymouth,* crowded with pioneers. There would be single men and there would be families with children . . . and she and Brian and Ngora were tangled up in tribal marriage battles. Frustrating, ridiculous, tragic.

Her eyes focused on the Kovas before her, seeing them again as she had first seen them before she had grown accustomed to them. Seeing their enormous buglike eyes varying green to yellow in their black fuzzy faces. Those faces were excited and curious. Conversation buzzed, black arms waved, cream-colored bodies jostled for good positions. And the men all wore swords and knives in their harness, waist belt and shoulder belt, and wore nothing else but their pouches, hanging in front like a Scotsman's sporran.

She was still alone inside the circle, no contestants, and it must be near time. As soon as the signal was given, no additional competitor could enter. Where was Brian?

There was a stirring of the crowd at one point. A burly long-armed Kovas shouldered through, sword already in one hand, round shield covering his other arm, black head rounded like the nose of a bomb, but with cat ears erect on each side. His bulbous eyes shone bright. His mouth showed a vacuous grin. Ogum, the Sukota who had often jerked her around when she wore her prisoner's puno collar! She shuddered.

A moment later she heard shuffling in the crowd behind her. Brian? No, another Kovas, one she had not noticed before. He was smaller than Ogum, compact, stepping quickly, face intense, body poised, taut, eager. The wings of his broad nose quivered with excitement. He stepped directly to Ogum. They slapped hands in greeting, then stood side by side, round leather shields on their left arms, right hands on their swords. Companions! Where is Brian?

A third Kovas pushed through, stared from Mirren to the other two. His heavy brow projected above his yellowish eyes. A lump of cheekbone projected below. His tongue licked his thick lips. His fist gripped on the hilt of the heavy sword hanging from his belt. Immediately came another with identical features. Twins! Where is Brian?

Her confidence was slipping. She felt a rusty tightness in her throat. She wanted to wipe the dampness of her palms on the legs of her uniform trousers, but she held back. It would betray her poise. What if her ending was to take care of a pair of furry nomadic husbands and their gray-felted hut? The *Plymouth* seemed in a different world, an unreal world. This was reality.

Thirty meters away, Ngora stood square on solidly planted feet, product of Haryal medical, one of earth's finest. Ignoring the crowd, she thought of her husband Chugar, who had not survived the crash landing on Vassa. And she thought back to Earth, back to ancestors chained to such posts as this, offered for sale. She had come a long way in time and space. She still had a way to go.

She eyed the crowd. Many of them she knew— Sukota she had doctored. She had no instruments, no drugs, but she had knowledge. She picked up local remedies, herbals and folklore. Life on Vassa was not so different that she could not take care of common problems, cuts, contusions, broken bones. Her thoughts were stopped by the entrance of two pairs of Kovas. She had doctored all of them for knife wounds. And maybe Rataq would stay away. His chances would be slim against these Kovas, sturdy warriors all. If that was what life was going to deal, she could cope. Also if the Old Litani are sending an army, that means the *Plymouth* is not yet destroyed. Maybe somewhere there is hope.

She heaved a sigh from her massive chest, looked at the sky. Except for momentary dark blue patches, a wind drove ragged clouds across the valley, tearing them away from high mountain peaks. Their colors shifted from bleached pink overhead through shades of dirty reddish gray to angry purples. Anything could happen.

Inibek strode into the group around Oveda's assigned post. He wondered that they were so few. The circle was empty! No Oveda! Where was she? Inibek halted, bewildered.

A Kovas on a stocky grybin, carrying a burning torch, dashed along the line of posts just outside the circles of spectators. The signal! "Nyada!

Nyada besega!" he called.

The love battles now begin.

At that moment Rataq burst through the crowd, stood panting in the open. The two pairs of Kovas looked over his slight figure, then fell on each other, slashing, parrying. Very plainly each had indicated, he does not look like much. We'll take care of him when we defeat the dangerous ones.

As the signal torch passed, Mirren saw Brian step through the packed Kovas surrounding her. The four warriors looked at Brian, looked at each other. Then they all turned toward Brian.

He recognized Ogum, the Sukota who had jerked him down by his puno collar. Brian grinned at him as he unsheathed his Vanth Nugol. He would enjoy.

Mirren gasped. All four at once. Soon Brian was fighting wildly, fend, dodge, sidestep, parry, beat off a snaking blade, whipping his two-handed sword high, low, side to side.

Mirren could not breathe. Everything inside stopped moving, benumbed. The four attackers separated, sidling around to beset him two on each side, confident now. They were sure to get him. Mirren saw Brian trip and go down. He tucked and rolled between the Kovas, bounced up just in front of Mirren, sweat on his forehead, a laugh on his lips.

Quickly he slued around, darted to his left, and for a moment he had a twin isolated one on one. His two-handed sword flashed, and cleaved layers of hardened wobargu hide. The shield was destroyed, but he had not reached the Kovas. No time for another swing. He dashed around Mirren and the post.

On the other side Mirren saw the companion of Ogum waiting, weapon ready. In full stride Brian closed on him, sword swinging. The heavy blade, with all Brian's weight and drive carrying it, smashed away the defending sword, glanced against the side of his head, sliced deep into his shoulder.

Now Mirren caught sight of the twin with the broken shield racing around her. She was frozen tight inside, but she heard her voice yell, "At your back!"

Brian wheeled in time to catch blade on blade. They strained for an instant, face to face. The second twin scorched around the post, leaping over Ogum's companion's fallen body.

Mirren was on fire, screaming again, "Behind you!" She was waving her arms, jumping up and down, wishing for a weapon. "Behind you!"

Brian thrust a leg behind the first twin. A quick heave flung him to the ground. Brian whirled to meet twin number two, whirled sword still extended, crouching low to escape a slash at his head. His blade cut in under the attacker's arm. But the turning carried him around with his back to Ogum. A cutting edge clawed across his back. His back ached, muscles convulsed. His spin continued around until he faced Ogum. Anger fought through pain.

"Your back!" Mirren cried out.

Later, my back. I still have this one to take.

Rataq paused in the circle of Kovas around Ngora, alert, one foot advanced slightly, weight balanced, ready, sword gripped tightly—too tightly, his hand trembled—round shield on his left arm. Awkward. He had never fought with a shield before. He had never fought a duel.

The two pairs of Kovas fenced furiously. Cuts, thrusts, parries, blades beating on shields. They paid no attention to Rataq.

Behind him in the crowd Rataq heard a titter.

His dark face flushed darker. Absurd position. Faculties peaked for battle. Ignored. Laughed at. He glared at the crowd.

Ngora called, "Rataq, come, stand by me."

He stalked toward her, watching the combatants. Rapidly the realization came that he was no match. He was quick, lithe, stronger, in better condition than he had ever been, but he had not the years of combat. He shivered. His hand touched the blaster at his belt. He could not use that in this duel. Or could he?

"Thank you for coming. The survivors will be weary, maybe wounded. Perhaps. . . ."

Rataq, eyes glued to fighting Kovas, burned for just that.

Then suddenly one Kovas was down on hands and knees, a leg dragging useless, his sword lying abandoned. The winner leaped to aid his companion against the remaining one. Soon he too lay bleeding on the grass.

Again Rataq lifted his shield and sword, crouched tensed, steady, tasted the sweat that rolled down his face.

The two Kovas relaxed side by side, panting. Red tongues lolled from between white teeth. But Kovas always panted when they were warm. They had no sweat glands under their fur. Panting did not mean exhaustion.

The smaller one spoke. "He's the one stole Pukar's Kel-Ufar, Skedre. I'll get him and the Kel."

"Do it, then, Skolo."

Like a snapped spring Rataq leaped, flailed with his blade and made Skolo give ground.

Skedre laughed. "Come on, big klugon sticker, finish him off. If I have to help, I'm first." He strode to Ngora, speared her eye with his. "Good times are coming." He smiled broadly. His breath smelled of kukri.

Ngora turned her head.

He grasped her jaw between thumb and fingers, forced her to look at him.

Her eyes blazed. "Desist!" she rasped with such intensity that Skedre recoiled.

Rataq drove in, hacking, but always his blade met the shield, was parried by the sword. The Kovas was playing with him, waiting until he wore himself out.

Skedre called, "Get it over with or I'll settle it." He jerked out his sword and stepped toward Rataq.

In a wild motion, Ngora swing her heavy fist backhanded. It cracked against his ear, knocked him flat.

For a moment Rataq's opponent gazed in suprise. Rataq pounced. This time his thrust broke through. Wounded, Skolo dropped to one knee.

A raider came wildly riding along the chain of circles. "Hear me. Hear me! This is the call of Inibek Kob. An army of Thana has broken through the pass. They are upon us! An army of Thana. . . ." His voice faded as he rushed by.

In the moment of stunned silence Ogum charged.

Mirren had never taken her eyes from the combat. "Brian!" she gasped.

He swung around to see a sword plunging toward his chest. No time to lift Vanth Nugol. He fell away, twisting. The blade followed downward, slithered across his skin. Now lying on his back, he thrust between the legs that were running over him. Ogum fell heavily. Brian bounded up, ready. Ogum lay stunned, waiting for Brian's final blow.

Brian held up. "The Kovas have need of you against the attack."

Ogum rose slowly. "I heard," he mumbled. "Thana, never before. . . ."

Other Nyada battlers heard, halted, stared at each other. With firm set lips they sheathed their weapons, ran for their grybins. The women ran for their tribal camps.

The girls at the stakes stood abandoned. Then they too ran for their own tribal areas, except Mirren and Ngora.

## seventeen

At the Nyada the Kovas could react quickly. They never left their torkas without weapons, swords hanging from their belts, quivers and bows lashed to their saddle pads, and wherever they fared their grybins were tethered nearby. And the Kovas knew their weapons; they had grown up with them in their hands. They knew their tactics, devised and polished in innumerable intertribal skirmishes. Still, they seemed like a disorganized rabble as they streamed down the valley toward the invaders.

Brian and Rataq rode double with Mirren and Ngora. Beside them, urging on his mount, rode Ogum. The streak of jagged pain across Brian's back dug deeper with every hoofbeat. His mind floated along somewhere above the great gnarl of pain that was his body, having no control, continually trying to grapple with the problem of how could they halt the fighting. It was Mirren's arms tight around him—she held the rein—that kept him on the saddle pad.

As they heard ahead of them the battle voice, Rataq raced toward a rise against the cliff at one side of the valley floor. Mirren followed. Ogum bore straight toward the action. On top of the rise, when Mirren slid off the grybin, the front of her uniform was smeared with blood. Brian fell off into her arms.

"Ngora, can you do something?" she pleaded.

Together they laid him flat. Ngora felt along the cut with gentle fingers. "Bleeding clean and not too deep." She pulled out a koana-leather pouch that hung from a thong about her neck. Mirren sat beside Brian, using his knife to cut off the legs of her uniform at midthigh. Ngora smeared on the native herbal salve, knotted the leg pieces together and bound Brian about the body.

He struggled to rise.

"No!" cautioned Ngora. "Here, we will prop you against the cliff."

There he sat, high enough to see the Thana army spread out below deployed in battle formation, advancing steadily. Already they had overrun the Kiyatagu camp. Brian watched the phalanx, pikemen six rows deep, a wall of glittering steel points stretching more than halfway across the valley. Behind them marched rows of bowmen, bows strung, arrows ready. On each flank were more bowmen many ranks deep. Beyond the archers on each side rode Thana cavalry. Not many, Brian thought, because few Thana had yet learned to fight on grybin back. The whole body seemed like some weird stretched-out insect moving sideways, wavy, sinuous, thicker at each end where head and tail brushed against the cliffs on each side of the valley.

Behind the formation rode groups of Litani officers. They wore no armor, either leather or mail, no shields, only their silver-gray Litani uniforms. They had no weapons he could see at a distance, but he knew they carried laser arms on their hips. Following after the officers came massed companies of Thana, reserves, pikemen and archers.

Rataq spoke with approval. "See, organization, discipline, in just a few weeks. That's what control can do."

Brian exploded, but his voice came out only a ghost of a roar. "Blast control! I taught the Thana that formation. I showed them how to fight a battle." He turned toward Rataq with a grimace of pain. "I want you to understand, these are my people. These are the people who picked me up, an alien crashed on their planet. I was alone, dying. They hid me from the Vanth, saved me. And when I learned they were held almost as slaves by the Vanth, I helped them overthrow. These are my people under new masters hunting me down. I'll not give myself up to the likes of that. We need a way to separate them from those new masters." He stopped with Ngora's quieting hand on his shoulder.

"We will be the new masters," Rataq declared.

Brian swore. "No masters! Thana will be free!"

Ngora stood, one hand on Brian's shoulder, and took Rataq's arm with the other. "Remember we are allies."

Rataq shrugged and smiled.

Brian's gaze returned to the valley below, saw the battle developing. He groped in his mind for some way to slow it down, but already both sides were committed. It would be like trying to stop a raging fire with an eye dropper, and he could barely move.

As the first small group of Kovas approached the advancing army, they veered to sweep back and forth across the path of the Thana, just out of bowshot. A few made little starts toward the Thana wall, hesitated and turned back.

The army still rolled on relentlessly, lines breaking up momentarily for uneven ground or a massive boulder, but reforming quickly, dressing the lines, pressing on.

"They will sweep the valley from end to end," Rataq exclaimed.

Brian's mind was in turmoil. He was proud of his Thana, yet it was necessary for the Kovas to stop them. What could he do, chained by his wound? He worked his back muscles. At least the pain was ebbing, but he felt a great lassitude. "These Kovas are warriors. They will do something," he said.

More and more Kovas raced to the battlefield—Kiyatagu, Juro, Sukota, Buka, all mounted, circling just out of Thana reach. In the dust rising from the pounding of many hooves, Brian could see the figure of Inibek Kob in their midst.

Above the beating of those hooves, muffled by distance, Brian heard saddle drums throbbing, heard Inibek's long-drawn-out wordless cry, "Kiya-a-a-a" taken up quickly by all the Kovas.

Now the Thana slowed and lowered long steel-pointed pikes to the ready. Each man edged a little to his right to be closer to the shield each one wore on his left arm. The line tightened into solid shields, pikes thrusting out between, heads peering over.

Milling Kovas became a unified horde thundering toward waiting Thana. Masses roared the war cry, the first note low, the second a high scream fading downward. "Kiya-a-a-a, kiya-a-a-a." They blistered the air.

Thana front rows jammed the butts of pikes into the ground, lowered the points breast high to the grybins, braced for the shock. Arrows arched from bowmen on the flanks and rear.

Kovas scorched onward, bowmen in the van, guiding grybins with their knees, and sprayed arrows from short powerful reflex bows. They shot, nocked the next arrow, shot again. Four arrows each Kovas loosed while riding forward. Brushing pike points, agile grybins wheeled in twisting leaps, reversed. Kovas archers slued around on their saddle pads, fired three more shafts as they raced away.

Steel points thunked on shields and helmets, but leather byrnies did not protect from the flying missiles that skimmed past the shields. Pikemen staggered back with feathered bolts quivering in necks and faces.

Oncoming Kovas lancers opened channels between them for Kovas bowmen's retreat. Lancers drove at the breaks in the pikepoints where Thana had fallen. The Thana shield line reeled from the shock of plunging Kovas lances. Rear ranks of pikemen rushed to fill the breaks to buttress the pike wall. Lancers probed but fell back, wheeled, retreated.

Thana archers again poured arrows into Kovas. Grybins screamed and fell, biting at piercing shafts. Kovas fell with their mounts. And spotted here and there, other Kovas fell from the cut of burning beams. Smells of burning flesh rose on the air.

"It's slaughter," Ngora whispered.

Whipping up from far reaches of the valley, more Kovas arrived. A second time they charged, Xergin and Togrel leading, along with Inibek Kob. Again ragged openings in the pike fence wall opened and closed. Kovas this time barely touched the steel line with their lances, faltered, wheeled, fled, this time in frayed formation, grybins ill controlled, stumbling.

Now the few Thana cavalry in their mail charged the retreating mob. Pikemen dashed forward in pursuit, dropping pikes, pulling swords, screaming, "Catch. Kill. Catch. Kill."

Farther and farther from the ranks they ran. A

staccato beat from saddle drums punched through battle noise. Kovas riders, suddenly in full control of their mounts, swung around and slashed with sabers at Thana on foot. They assailed Thana riders, drove toward the jumbled shield wall. Then came laser fire, picking off Kovas riders until they retreated in earnest.

Brian groaned. It was slaughter for both sides.

The afternoon crawled agonizingly away. Kovas charges dragged further and further apart. Stabbing beams of burning colored light cut down more Kovas and grybins than did the flights of Thana arrows. And always the Thana pressed onward. When the yann, blood red, disappeared behind the western ridges, and the combatants disengaged, the Kiyatagu area was totally in Thana hands. They were closing in on the Juro camp. The watchers fled toward the Sukota lodges.

As they approached Xergin's torka, Brian recognized the bodyguards of all the deitches before the entrance. A high-level meeting was already in session.

Ogum stepped out from the group, grinning savagely. "You come." He beckoned. His manner had implications.

Why is he so happy, Brian wondered. Stiffly he walked after him. Rataq followed, but Mirren and Ngora were stopped by other guards before the doorway.

As the doorflap dropped behind them, all talk ceased. The flickering light from the central fire was the only light in the smoke-filled room. The sucking of flames at the wood was the only sound. In the flamelight and shadow that fluttered across the faces of the deitches, where they sat on a row of chests against the curve of the opposite torka wall, Brian saw all eyes turned toward them. In the center were Xergin and Togrel of the Sukota, then

Khalid and Hizim of the Juro, and on the other side Yafi and Qais of the Buka. Looking grim, Inibek was standing before them. Brian and Rataq stepped to the edge of the fire beside Kors and Cogbard. Brian smelled tension in the smoky air. They were trapped, all of them, but he could not guess why.

Behind Brian a guard said, "We have the women. We hold them outside."

"So." Xergin nodded, satisfaction showing in his voice. "We have them all."

In the pause that followed, Inibek Kob pointed at Brian. "Speak for yourself now. Why are you here?" His voice was strained.

Why that question? Brian searched the faces. What has changed? What has gone wrong? "The Thana have your camp. We brought the women here...."

Kob cut him off. "No, not that. Why are you in our land, the Kovas' land?"

Brian stared. He scratched his chin through his red beard while his thoughts scrambled for the best answer. What was the purpose? Slowly he said, "We sought refuge from the Litanofoq."

Khalid of the Juro spoke. "If this is true and if the Thana and the Litani are genuinely here to seize them, we should hand them over. Their purpose accomplished, they will leave our land."

Inibek growled, "When did we, Kovas, ever surrender our guests to an enemy?"

Xergin held up his hand. "Idle argument. These are spies. They are Litanofoq, people of little eyes—all of them except those two Thana they have bought. They came here to find us and direct their army. Did any of them fight with us today? Did you tell us—" he thrust an accusing finger toward Inibek—"how Litani came in a box that flies? And this one—" he pointed now at Rataq—

"went away with them and later he came back again?

"Also this one—" he fingered Cogbard—"how did he come to our land? All entrances were watched. He came not through any of them, yet here he is. The box that flies? That army came here swiftly and directly after we withdrew our watches at the gateways. Spies know how to send messages."

Rataq quickly dropped his hand away from the chain and jewel he had been fingering.

Silence again with firelight flicking across dark furry faces. Tiny gleams glittered from multiple facets. Inibek stood with huge hands on hips, head forward thrust. He gazed along the curve, Qais, Yafi, Togrel, Xergin, Khalid and Hizim.

"Do you remember," Kob spoke slowly, softly, "that not more than three days ago I sent you word of a report there was a Thana army approaching? You laughed." He beat his fist on his chest. "I too did not believe. I sent only two Kovas to watch the passage." Now his voice cut the air. "Two hundred would have stopped them. Do you know who warned?" He brought his hand around to Brian and Rataq. "It was they. Is that an act of a spy?"

"A spy's coverup when he knows it is too late to act," sneered Xergin.

Inibek glared. "I know these men. We escaped together from your camp, deitch of the Sukota. We have ridden together, fought together, lived in the same torka. These are not spies."

"Rackeris! Smoke only that stings the eyes." Qais spat on the matter before him. "Better we take off their heads and be done. Our problem is tomorrow. We care little about yesterday. These Litani have terrible weapons, burning far-kill weapons. Do we fight tomorrow or do we leave the valley tonight? There are many ways not closed to us."

Out of the corner of his eye Brian saw Rataq's hand move to his blaster. He reached for Rataq's wrist, gripped it—gripped it too tight, fighting the rush of fear inside him.

A log on the fire shifted and flame blazed, lighted the stern set of Kovas faces before him. But an idea had caught fire in Brian's brain. All afternoon, agonizing through the battle, he had strained for a workable idea and had found none. Now here it was, simple, easy, flawless.

"I can tell you a way to stop the Thana." His voice was overloud in his ears. He softened it. "And I can tell you how to capture those Litani with their far-kill weapons."

Xergin snapped, "Spies giving advice. Beware."

Brian held silent for a long pause, feeling their attention, in his mind testing his idea. Could he sell it to this hostile audience? Slowly he began, forcing confidence into his voice. "Tomorrow is the day of your Tsuring ceremony. Your herbal fires are laid and ready but unlit. They stretch across the valley near the river." He studied the faces before him.

"There you have the means, and you are master of the valley, masters of the Kovas world. Your great spirit, the spirit of Nalpur of Runn provides the way. Listen now. In the morning, give way slowly. Cross the river when the yann is high. Hold there until the wind comes, the wind that every day sweeps down from the peaks through the valley a little after the yann passes its height. Then light your fires, retire quickly upwind. The Thana and the Litani crossing the river will breath deep of the smoke and the fragrance of the tangri. Soon they will be helpless. Then go in, take their weapons and bind the Litani, and you have conquered. The battle is done."

The faces of the deitches froze in horror. There was a confusion of voices. "Never! Never! Use the sacred fire in war! Never!"

Xergin dominated. "Sacrilege! Painful death for the spies. But we have little time. It must be quick."

Inibek jerked his sword from its scabbard, faced the seated deitches. "It is I you must kill first. Have at me!"

No one moved.

## *eighteen*

Brian shivered in the early dawn light. Wrapped in their cloaks, he and Rataq had spent the night in the open. Inibek had led Brian, Rataq and the women away from Xergin's torka—no one stopped him—to camp near the river with as many Kiyatagu as he could gather. The two Thana, Kors and Cogbard, remained prisoners.

Brian pushed himself up against the darting pang that hacked across his back. Motionless, gazing at the bloody red of the east silhouetting the jagged black line of mountains, he waited for the pain to subside. Something glinted high in the air. He touched Rataq's shoulder.

Started out of sleep, he bounced to his feet in one convulsive jump, sword in hand.

Brian chuckled. "Mighty quick this morning. Take a look." He pointed just above the swirling peak of Runn.

Rataq followed the point. It was plain now, an air car dropped down to land among the red glitter atop the black frozen flame tips.

"Why do they land?" Brian asked. "They could direct the battle better hovering above."

"They did not conquer the valley in a half-day sweep. They desire a decisive advantage." He squinted at the movements he could see at the lip of the cliff, tiny figures perhaps unloading something. "I believe they are emplacing a belyan."

"Belyan?"

"Something like what you call a laser, like my blaster, but larger, with greater power and range. From up there it will destroy the Kovas. If that is what they are doing, they will need a second trip for the primary power supply. The air car cannot carry both on one trip."

They watched and waited while on a flat rock heated in an early morning fire Mirren and Ngora cooked a crackerlike loggets bread.

Inibek appeared with Oarda, still searching for Oveda and his boys. "What do you watch?" he asked, peering.

"An air car there on the mountain."

Just then it lifted to wing away. "I think we need to get up there to the top," Brian said.

"I see no box that flies. And no man climbs that mountain. That is Altar Runn, the mountain of Nalpur of Runn. No man climbs that mountain."

Brian opened his mouth, then closed it again. His thought was that with some good hard-rock gear he could climb that mountain, but it would take all day. And he had no climbing gear, nor did he have all day. He groaned at the thought of the slaughter. The Kovas would be decimated.

Into the long pause Rataq spoke slowly, as much to himself as to the others. "I believe I know that mountain, I have never seen it from the valley until now, but I think I have seen it from the air. And I have seen labs inside."

"Your microtapes?" exclaimed Brian.

"Exactly. Boroc Eichen, Laf Yyon, Aiten Napr, Belyo Belyan—they all worked here on an early development using light from yann, the ancestor of our blasters, our heat rays. That's a misnomer.

It is not a heat ray so much as a light ray, concentrated, powerful in the high-frequency end of the light spectrum. Whatever it hits bursts into flame, not from heat but from pure quantum energies, photons run wild."

"But yann is primarily in the red spectrum."

"There is enough in the high frequencies, and there is more energy potential there than in the lows. On our long cruise we refined those early experiments. I have my blaster." He slapped his hip.

Inibek looked sharply at Rataq. "I do not understand all that talk. But this is the weapon that burns?" His great hands clenched at his sides. "You did not fight with us yesterday."

Rataq looked away toward Runn and back again. "You are right. I should have been there."

"Today you will."

"One blaster is insufficient against their many. Today it is more needful that I get to the top of Runn."

"No man climbs that mountain. But now both of you want to climb." He shook his head. "Why?"

Rataq explained. "A great blaster is on top."

Brian added, "Remember how my eyes could see the Sukota coming long before you could?"

"I remember, but no man climbs our sacred mountain."

Rataq pulled his blaster. "I can set it—" he thumbed a small knob—"to cut like a hot knife." He pointed the weapon at a small tree by the river; a narrow gash exploded. The tree toppled. "Or I can set it to cover a large area." He thumbed again. A large bush ten meters away burst into crackling flame.

"Inibek, will you allow the giant blaster like this up there? It will burn this whole valley like that spot on the hill you showed us."

Inibek's shoulders sagged. He seemed to shrink. "No man climbs the mountain of Runn," he mumbled.

"Litani are there," Brian said.

Rataq touched Inibek's arm. "We will not climb it. We will go inside. There must be a way."

"Aliens inside! No!" He grasped Rataq's wrist in a big paw. "No one but Kovas men. No women. No aliens."

Rataq's other hand was on his blaster.

Quietly Brian said, "We have to go."

Inibek dropped Rataq's wrist and glared at Brian.

A smallish figure approached them, fur matted, crusted with dirt, body sagging with fatigue. Now it was beginning to run, staggering. A small voice called weakly, "Father, most honored father." The standard polite address from children.

Inibek turned, ran to meet Ekai.

"Father," there was sobbing in his voice. "Mother and Alungo never came out."

"Oveda, Alungo! Tell me." He knelt, wrapped strong arms about the boy, held him close. "Now tell me."

Ekai told how he and Alungo had wanted to show their deep feeling for Benjak. It was the son's proper duty to place shumshuls in the sacred caves of Runn. Oarda tagged along, but they would not let her go in. She ran away looking for father Kob.

"She must have found not me, but Oveda, before the Nyada began," muttered Inibek.

Ekai told how they were attacked and how they fought. He showed the acid burns on his shoulder and arm. Ekai was trying to tear grutmauls away from Alungo when Oveda got there. Together they ripped away the grutmauls. Oveda picked up Alungo. Oveda made Ekai run ahead for help. But there was a battle. No one would come. Oveda and

Alungo never came out.

"Oh, honorable father, it was all my fault. I could have stopped Alungo. I could have." His chest heaved in sobs.

Inibek held him against his breast, silent for a long while. Finally he spoke. "Not you but I am responsible. You are my family, mine and Benjak's. I have loved the hunt, ridden down the chladni, speared the klugon. I have loved the raids, the battles, meeting a foe sword to sword. Better I should have taught the children at my knee."

"Oh, honorable father. It is I. . . ."

"Enough! You do not gainsay your father. Now go to the camp yonder. The first woman you see, show her your shoulder. She will know how to make a salve for it. Go now! The acid eats and does not stop. Then you seek out Tulu and Radja. They will be your protectors if I do not return."

"But Father!"

"I go with these men. Here." He undid his belt, stripped off his harness with its heavy sword. "You will be deitch. Go!" He shoved Ekai toward the camp and turned his back.

Ekai turned slowly, then stumbled away, carrying the sword in both hands.

"We will help you find Oveda," Brian said.

"She is lost. The mountain does not release a woman. She knew." He straightened up, staring at the mountain. "Come, let us get our grybins." He walked toward the tethered animals unsteadily, suddenly an old man.

Just inside the entry, Inibek applied flint and steel to the torches, one for each. His motions were slow, his bulky body slack. The simple task seemed a great effort for him. As the torches flared, Brian saw the red light pick out the piles of shamshuls in the corners. This was the day when they lit the Tsuring fires, the final farewell to the dead, and the men carried the votive tablets into the caves to leave them forever in its protection.

Brian glanced at Inibek, vacant eyed, listless. Family tragedy or not, they needed Inibek alert, active, aggressive.

Rataq was scrutinizing the walls between the passage openings, holding his torch high, studying colored patterns etched into the slick black glassy surface. Dimmed by centuries, there was still a discernible grid of many colors with swirling markings in and around it. Rataq's free hand traced along the lines, his face rapt. He moved from one figure to the next. "Yes," he said, "it is as I thought. These are the layouts of the caves, the excavation—the terscien—we call it, all melted out and making that wide ramp up to the entry. They already had simple heat rays in those days and were seeking devices with more power and precision. Nine levels. Here's the entry." He stepped to the end where he had begun. "And the halls, rooms, offices, libraries, data processing, the labs, mechanical, electronic, materials, optics, prototype shops. A complete research facility. But the passages between levels? Must be at the very top where the lines fade away." He paused, gazing upward. "We go straight to the rear. There must be a shaft."

They belted their leather robes around them with harnesses and swords outside, pulled the hoods over their heads.

Inibek growled, "You should not bring your weapons. The caves are holy."

Brian considered, hand on the hilt of Vanth Nugol. He shook his head.

"Alungo carried his sword. He did not come back."

"I keep my weapon," Brian said. Rataq nodded in agreement.

"The mountain of Runn is sacred and it defends itself. We shall see. Weapons and women are not permitted. But—" he shrugged— "you are warned."

Warned is right, Brian thought. Sacred, holy it is not. It is evil, malevolent. It swallows people, black cave of the dead. We must get through it quickly.

Inibek led the way into the center passage where Rataq pointed. In the flickering light, doorways showed the great thickness of the walls. Doors, probably wooden, had powdered to dust, but hinges were still bright and sturdy, formed of some chemically inert metallic material and spiked into the rock with the same substance.

In the thick dust on the floor there were tracks. Brian bent down to look. "Three going in, one coming out."

Inibek stared down at the marks. He moaned, shook himself, started at a half run along the passage, sweeping his torch close to the ceiling as he went, letting the flames scorch up into the cracks. Brian and Rataq followed quickly.

A small grutmaul dropped out of one crack and writhed on the floor, arms twisting about in agony. Inibek smashed a heel down on it viciously. "I cannot fight the mountain, but I kill grutmauls."

Farther on, from a larger rift, three dropped down. Two squirmed on the floor, but one, hardly touched by the flames, clung to Rataq's head. He yelled as an arm swung across his face.

Brian jabbed it away with his sword, stamped on it, felt its pulpy body under his boot.

They hurried by more doorways, saw ranks of machinery stretching away into the dark, saw benches and tables of the same bright enduring metal, and everywhere shumshuls on tables, benches, on the flat tops of the machines.

They reached the first great fissure across the floor, an easy jump. But there on the other side lay scattered teeth and some bits of bones.

Inibek stopped short with a great wordless, almost wailing sound.

Brian spoke. "It can't be. Only bits of bones."

Suddenly they were inundated by a flood of grutmauls—small ones, forearm's length to larger ones a full arm's length across, all flopping down on them from the fissure overhead.

They fought, jabbing and thrusting with torches and swords, stamping on grutmauls that fell to the floor. Each knocked grutmauls off the others' heads and backs. The acrid smell rose of mixed smoke and burned flesh, and cutting through was the vapor of stomach acids attacking leather robes.

Rataq screamed, threw down his torch and sword, tore with his hands at the grutmaul covering his face. Inibek thrust his torch into the body until, thrashing and jerking, it dropped away. The torch flared bright in the acids.

As Rataq stooped to recover sword and torch, Brian burned another grutmaul from his back. As they fought they kept moving away from the huge crack and the smashed grutmauls searing in their own acids.

Inibek stopped to look at Rataq's face. "Only a small spot of acid, spemzal, on your forehead. It will eat to the bone, but it will heal. The spemzal smeared on our robes burns slowly, but soon we must throw them down. The moment you feel a bite, take off your robe."

They continued at a fast walk until they saw the black shiny wall at the end of the passage. They reached it. Halls led away to the right and left.

"There is a shaft somewhere," Rataq exclaimed. "There must be."

They found it offset to the right, a square shaft with a notch in the corner containing a ladder that extended upward into the black. Brian gripped a rung of the cold metal, shook it. It seemed solid, made of the same bright enduring metal.

"Nine levels?"

"Much more," Rataq said. "That is only what they tersciened. There will be many meters of solid rock to the top of the mountain."

They dropped their acid-smeared robes, and Inibek started up, one hand for the torch, one hand for the ladder. As he climbed Brian noticed that the callused bare feet of Inibek were red with acid burns. But Inibek climbed steadily.

When Kob was high enough to clear the leaping flames of his torch, Rataq began his climb. As Brian reached to haul his weight up the first step, an arc of pain stabbed across his back. He held still on the first rung, breathing deep. Finally he climbed, one hand for the torch, the other on the ladder for balance only. All climbing he did with his legs. Now the rounded rungs pressed into the arches of his feet. The soles of his boots were paper thin. He remembered all the grutmauls he had stamped. How long would it take that acid to eat through? He thought about the gnawing on the soles of Inibek's feet.

At level five they took a short breather, and at level nine again, where Rataq discovered a middle-sized grutmaul creeping toward them along the floor. They burned it, began the long climb.

Brian's back was lashed across by a stripe of fire. His feet were an agony. Each step crushed flesh into bones. Then at eye level he saw something that obliterated the agony—a thick grutmaul arm extending from a fissure behind the ladder. Hooks and suckers reached toward his face. He could not bring his torch down so close. He almost ran up the ladder until he heard Rataq shout.

"Torch! Torch!"

Brian stopped short until Rataq climbed away. Then farther above he heard gasping words.

"Great Nalpur, help me!"

A torch fell past Brian, flaring until it shrank to a speck down the long shaft. He could hear wheezing struggle, but he could not see past Rataq, who was partway off the ladder, jabbing with his torch. Crowding upward, Brian finally saw the great gray arm that circled Inibek's shoulders, another that crawled around one arm. He gripped and shook the ladder in a frenzy; he could not reach anything else. But now he could see the huge crack into which the mother of grutmauls hauled Inibek. A great split in the solid rock had wrenched the ladder apart.

Inibek was off the ladder and Rataq scrambled fully into the split, burning, thrusting, hacking at the central body. Brian reached from the end of the ladder, ramming his torch at flailing arms. Grutmaul flesh sizzled; bitter acrid smoke seared his nose, scalded his eyes. He could see the thickened middle section hunched down on Inibek's shoulder. He knew the stomach was exuding its dissolving acids. He chopped with his sword at the arm that seized Rataq's leg.

Then it was over. Rataq hacked straight through the center of its nervous system. Its arms fell away, writhing aimlessly.

Brian and Rataq hauled the flabby stinging body parts away from Inibek, dumped them down the shaft. They could do nothing with the viscous corrosive mucous that covered his shoulder and the side of his head. Wiping did not remove it, only smeared it.

Brian's eyes met Rataq's in the smoky light. His guts twisting like the grutmaul's arms, Brian made the decision. "Damn! No way to carry him.

No use to stay." They dragged him back away from the slime. "We'll come back when we can," he said, but Inibek seemed unconscious.

With Brian holding his harness to steady him, Rataq reached for the bottom of the displaced ladder. He could barely reach it. He settled back against Brian, laid his torch on the rock.

"Need both hands."

Then, with a shove from Brian, he was securely on the ladder. Brian was taller, he reached the ladder, muscled his way up hand over hand, back muscles screaming until his feet found the bottom rung. He hung there until the trembling of his body relaxed. Somehow the pain helped him adjust to the thought of Inibek lying abandoned in the crevice. Finally he climbed into the dark above. Both torches lay sputtering on the rock beside Inibek Kob.

## *nineteen*

Knifelike rays of light sliced through the dark from narrow slits overhead, thin beams lighting only what they touched. Everything else lay in shadow. Rataq and Brian had reached the end of the ladder and crawled with aching muscles onto a metal platform. Brian's feet jerked in spasms. He undid the remnants of his boots to rub with his hands, while his eyes searched in the dimness for a way to the outside. Rataq lay at full length, breathing in fast shallow gasps.

After minutes, Brian rose to test his feet, felt the joy in them as they pressed against a flat surface. Prowling around the platform, he guessed that the long narrow slit was the center between a set of doors over the shaft. Tiny dots of light shone at one side where three steps led up to a small dirt-encrusted grating in some sort of a round cover. He stepped up to test it.

Rataq rolled over to sit up, then sprang to his feet, blaster ready.

Brian pressed upward, gently at first, feeling for some sign of movement. None. Cemented there by the centuries, he thought. He tried again, arms, shoulders, body straining. The cover popped up suddenly. Outside, there was a yell. Brian saw a reeling, stumbling Litani swinging around, a startled, incredulous look on his face and a blaster in his hand.

Brian jerked down the cover, felt the scorch of the blaster along his forearm. "Had to be standing on it," he said. "So much for surprise." He shrugged. "Maybe we can find how to open the big doors while they watch the little one."

"Those will be powered doors," said Rataq, "but there should be a manual override."

"Maybe this is it." Brian reached up beyond one end of a long slit of light to a large wheel extending from the wall.

Rataq stepped to the other end of the slit, aiming his blaster.

Brian strained at the wheel. There was a harsh grating sound. It turned slowly. Doors cracked apart a few centimeters, metal to metal that had not moved for centuries rasped and shrieked.

"So much for surprise again," muttered Brian.

He heard the crackle of Rataq's blaster.

Rataq grinned at Brian. "He was in the light. I was in shadow."

"Outside, before they recover," Brian commanded. He flung up the small cover, leaped out, sword in hand. Rataq followed closely. They gazed around expectantly at a confused forest of enormous upstanding crystals. Taller than a man and many of them thicker, gleaming with light, they projected from their dark matrix at random angles, horizontal to vertical in all directions, some of them murky, many of them clear, all of them with high reflectivity, both interior and exterior. Red light from the yann, high in the sky, bounced in all directions, breaking into a myriad of colors. Brian and Rataq were nearly blinded by the intensity.

Vulnerable, helpless, Brian wondered why they had not yet been blasted. More Litani surely were there hiding behind the crystal shafts. Squinting against the light, he could see the crumpled body of only the single man lying before the sliding doors.

There was no one in sight, only the appearance of a path winding away from where he stood into the crystal jungle. Cautiously, eyes slowly accommodating to the brightness, they started along the path.

"*Orendo, Orendo.*" They heard a call. "*Arinc eed gener tas.*"

Rataq whispered to Brian, "The generator has arrived. He is calling for Orendo to help unload."

The voice was coming closer. Brian and Rataq squeezed between angled crystals on opposite sides of the path. But the crystals were not opaque. As he rounded a corner, the Litani saw something, snatched his blaster from his belt.

Rataq was bringing his gun up to bear when it disintegrated from the Litani's shot.

With a roar, Brian leaped out.

Startled, dismayed by the great redbearded body hurling toward him, the Litani turned and ran. He turned the corner, shouting in a terrified voice, "Kovas! Kovas!"

Brian halted his rush. "So much for surprise, again," he muttered.

Rataq shook his stinging hand. They looked at each other, at the bits of broken blaster.

"Off the path," Brian commanded.

They scrambled in among the jumble of crystals. Far to the left they began to work their way along, parallel to the path. It was not really walking but climbing, in, around, through. The footing was at all angles. They used their arms as much as their feet.

They scrambled and climbed and crawled and squeezed under and through. It seemed three times the distance; the peak of Runn could not be large.

The sun was straight up, no help in fixing their direction. It burned down, the crystals caught it, threw it back or across at angles. Crossing such a beam, Brian felt the fiery intensity.

"That's not just reflection?"

"That's right. Here they discovered the principle that led to our blasters and the parser gun."

"But you can't add energy just by reflection."

"Touch that crystal on the back side away from the beam."

Brian felt a vibration. With his hand on the column he heard a humming.

"It is the light. These polyhedral crystals gather light. It bounces back and forth, different crystals resonate at different frequencies, they build. They separate microwaves and light into discrete groups: microwave, infrared, the colors and ultraviolet. These frequencies project out of windows in the crystals, amplified coherent beams. It seems random, of course, but there must be patterns depending on the incidence of the rays from the yann. At various times windows emit greater or less energy. It's like natural lasers. The greatest effect is at the high frequencies, concentrated energy. When the angles and right windows focus together on some point, molecules and atoms bang way up the scale of energy states. That point explodes into fire."

Brian stopped short. Directly before him a Litani trained a blaster on him point blank. He had not been paying attention. Damn the blast! I can't lose now. The *Plymouth*. Mirren. He tried to dive down flat but could not do it. He was held erect in the press of the close-packed hodgepodge of crystals.

The blaster beam spit.

Brian felt nothing.

Over to his right a thick crystal shattered. Shards crashed down. Why wasn't he hit? He forced himself to relax, to scan closely the figure with the blaster. It was a bit fuzzy, the outline broken in places. A reflection, he realized. An image bounced around among the crystals as in a funhouse of mirrors. When Brian finally moved, the figure disappeared. Then he heard a commanding voice.

Rataq translated. "He says to stop the useless firing. Get on with the generator. It's Ubeq's voice."

They took direction from the voices. In a few steps through the crisscross jumble of crystals, Brian could see Ubeq standing with his back to the cliff, facing a half circle of clearing with a blaster in his hand. Four Litani were wrestling the power generator from the air car.

Rataq whispered, "We can separate and charge him from two directions."

Ubeq heard and spun toward them. "Step out or I burn you right there." He advanced a step toward them.

Brian could almost feel the cauterizing beam. His arm felt again the grazing shot at the manhole. "Better stand and face it," he muttered. He rose, stepped slowly out. Rataq moved away so he could not be caught with the same shot.

Turko, a gloating smirk on his face, let them come on, eyeing them, finger tightening on the trigger. The four with the generator half out of the car stood silent, tense, holding the weight.

Arragh—arr—agh! Kiya-a-a." A great choking roar. Inibek Kob charged from the path. One side of his face was seared half away, his teeth showing through his cheek. One arm hung limp, the other was outstretched, with a great clutching hand. His lumbering run was lurching unevenly, but straight at Ubeq.

The blaster burned the air. The outstretched

hand and arm to the elbow crumpled in a blast of energy, but his body carried on.

Ubeq fired again. A blackening hole bored into Inibek's chest. Still he stumbled on. His shoulder smashed into Turko Ubeq. They fell over the side, both of them.

Brian recovered first. "At 'em." He rushed the four Litanis. They dropped their load, jerked at their blasters. With the first sweep of his sword he took off the arm of one, smashed into the chest of the second.

Rataq dove for the falling blaster. Shots cracked over his head. There was a strong smell of ozone.

Brian thrust over the generator. His sword burned hot in his hand, half sheared off. He flung the hilt in the face of the Litani, then struck at the arm that held the blaster, smashed it down on top of the machine. Firing from the ground, Rataq cut down the fourth Litani.

Quickly Brian ran to the edge of the cliff to sweep the valley with his gaze. Where was the battle?

Many still figures lay on the turf. The Kovas had retreated past the stream. They milled around on their grybins beyond the line of prepared piles of firewood salted with tengri herbs.

The Thana army was reforming after crossing the stream, reserves coming into position. Brian looked intently at the Kovas. Their formation yesterday had been loose, haphazard, but somehow purposive. At some precise moment it all linked together, merged into a coordinated attack. Now they were a confused rabble like ants from a disturbed nest. Individuals and small groups drifted away up the valley. Yesterday all movement was toward the battle.

"Kovas are breaking up, beginning to run," Brian exclaimed. "How soon can we get that belyan operating?"

"Soon." Rataq had no breath left for talk. "Give us a hand."

Lugged into position, cables connected. It was soon.

"Now what?"

"Fire those wood piles. Then watch for a fabulous sight."

Rataq trained the beam. One by one the piles burst into flame, smoky flame.

"Enough," said Brian. "We don't want them burning too fast."

Smoke drifted toward the stream and the Thana army.

The Kovas stopped their random riding and sat their mounts, watching.

The controlled Thana army began their advance. Dressing their lines carefully, they approached the line of smoky fires through the fragrant smoke that carried toward them on the light breeze. A few emerged to the windward side, found themselves outdistancing their formation, paused, shaking their heads, then stared around, vaguely bewildered. The rest continued from the stream, bunching together with the front ranks in the drifting smudge.

At cliff edge Brian peered intently. He saw the formation break into individuals or clumps of Thana, hanging onto each other. Some sat on the ground, weapons forgotten. Litani officers charged into the disorganization with angry drive.

Brian raised his head high, spread his arms wide. "We've done it!" he shouted. "We've done it."

A strange wind sound surged up from the Kovas. It was a sigh of relief. It was a sounded wordless prayer. They pointed and waved toward the great sacred fire mountain of Runn. Nalpur of Runn had saved them.

The Kovas dismounted, figures ran toward the

reeling Thana.

"Massacre!" Rataq yelled.

"No," said Brian. "They are collecting weapons."

Kovas darted in among the Thana, picking up the long spears, the shields, the bows and quivers of arrows, then running quickly back to load them on grybins.

"Rataq, I am forgetting. Communications. Can we raise the *Plymouth* with the radio?" He pointed to the air car.

"Right," answered Rataq, "we can try." In the car, he swept slowly across the frequencies that Brian suggested.

Loud and clear they heard a voice saying, "This is Brian McCann. This is Brian McCann. Beam down on this frequency. We have prepared a landing area for you."

Stunned, Brian stared at Rataq. "It's someone at Colufo, isn't it?"

"It is Eckem Meluq's voice relayed from Colufo." He flipped to transmit.

Brian was on the air. For many months and for longer than that, because the purpose of the entire scouting expedition was to help colonizers land, he had been striving for this moment, not always believing it could happen. Now here was the first ship, and he did not know what to say. How could he convince the *Plymouth* they were getting directions to destruction?

He tried. "Belay that direction!" he almost shouted. "It is false. It leads to a crash landing. That was not Brian McCann. This is Brian McCann. You can home in on this signal for a safe landing. Over."

Silence.

Brian repeated.

Silence. Then a sharp irritated voice: "How

many Brian McCanns do we have down there?"

"One, plus an imposter. That imposter is trying to get you to crash in the wild and jagged mountains. Here is a large flat field, ideal for your letdown."

Brian stuttered in frustration and rage. "What ... what ... what lands at Colufo, crashes at Colufo. That is an alien determined to control this planet. Ask him some questions about Earth."

Meluq's voice cut in. "Good idea. Here's a suggestion. What company is sending the *Plymouth* on this trip?" He answered his own question. "The Off-World Transport Corporation."

Brian's mind raced. How could he know that?

"Name the oceans on Earth." Again he answered himself. "Latlanty, Pacify, Indy, Arcty, Anaecty."

How can he know? How can he know? It flashed into Brian's mind. Mirren. When they had Mirren under control, they picked her brain, especially for information about Earth.

Brian almost shouted, "Beware of a man who answers only his own questions! *Plymouth,* have you detected an orbiting ship?"

"Yes. Tell us about it."

"The aliens came in it, landed, and have set a trap for you at Colufo. They forced both our ships to crash. This is why we could send no messages."

"Where are the other members of your expedition? Captain Johansen, Lieutenant Fitzgerald. . . ."

"All but Lieutenant Fitzgerald and Doctor Goroga were killed in the crashes. They are not here at the moment. I can get them later."

"Well, other Brian?"

"Just wait, I'll have them shortly."

Brian's mind whirled. What was Mirren totally unfamiliar with? Sports! "Change frequencies to the score of last year's Ulti-bowl game. Over."

Brian gave Rataq the numbers. He rolled thumb-wheels.

"*Plymouth, Plymouth.* Come in."

In moments they heard the voice from the *Plymouth*. In another moment they heard Eckem Meluq. "Here we all are. Tricky, isn't he. I wonder how he knew that number."

Rataq said, "His equipment sweeps frequencies in microseconds and locks onto radiation. No chance that way."

## twenty

As Rataq dropped the air car down to the valley floor in search of Mirren and Ngora, the Kovas scattered from beneath, forming a ring of mounted and dismounted warriors. For some time now Kovas had been staggering out from between the fires with shields, swords, helmets, tying them to saddle pads. Their faces were wild with the spirit of miraculous victory and rich booty, but their movements were increasingly loose and erratic.

Out from the circle Xergin stepped. "Ho, spy!" he called. "Nalpur laid you low, all of you. Now look at your army. They are no more than a little dust in the eyes, no more than a few magli droppings on stony ground. Now what use is your box that flies?" He shook a spear in his fist toward Brian.

Around him, lances were poised, arrows nocked on taut sinew. Rasping growls rose from many throats.

Blast them for idiots, Brian thought. Don't they know we just won the battle for them? But they did not know. Their short-range eyes could not distinguish what had happened on the mountaintop. Brian knew that.

"Back in!" Rataq cried.

"No!" Mirren and Ngora are in here somewhere.

Brazen it out. These guys are more drunk than dangerous."

Two figures on foot dashed through the clusters of Kovas—Kors and Cogbard, running with arms loaded with blasters. They tossed weapons to Brian. They stood, the three of them, two-fisted with blasters.

"Ridiculous!" said Brian.

Xergin let fly his spear. The ring of Kovas warriors pressed in closer behind him. The spear quivered in the ground a meter short.

Brian fired the spot of grass just in front of Xergin. He scrambled back.

Rataq called, "Everybody in! We will take off."

"No, no!" Kors burst out. "Mirren and Ngora were collecting blasters too. They will be here in moments."

A running figure burst through. It was not Mirren or Ngora. Blasters leveled.

"Hold!" Brian yelled.

The figure was not a charging warrior but a boy, Ekai. Brian dropped his weapons on the ground to receive Ekai in his arms.

Breathless, he choked out, "Honorable Father! You went away with Honorable Father. He is not back."

Brian held him close, "Your Honorable Father saved my life—our lives, all of us. He saved your people and he saved our people, ones who are coming. When there is time I will tell you. But know that he is a hero. There will be great songs to sing of Inibek Kob."

The radio crackled. "Well, what is the delay?"

Rataq answered, "McCann has gone to find Lieutenant Fitzgerald and Doctor Goroga."

"And who are you?"

"I . . . I am assisting Mr. McCann.

Outside the air car, Brian heard, but he kept his

eyes on the press of Kovas warriors. They had lowered their weapons, watching Ekai. Where was Mirren?

Again Eckem Meluq's voice came from the radio. "I have here Lieutenant Fitzgerald." A touch of gloat glittered in his voice.

A feminine voice spoke aggressively. "Lieutenant Fitzgerald here. To whom am I speaking?"

"Never mind that. Report your condition."

That tears it, Brian thought.

Then, hurrying through the massed Kovas, came Mirren and Ngora.

"On the double!" Brian shouted. "*Plymouth* on the radio. Into the car! Talk!"

Mirren stopped, one foot in the door, her hands on the frame. The feminine voice was still speaking. "Afterward we were able to establish a good rapport with the natives, though there are warrior tribes in the mountains who are still fighting. Beware of landing there. We have prepared a suitable field here at a small town called Colufo. We are ready now to assist you in setting down."

Mirren flashed a bewildered look over her shoulder at Brian.

"Imposter."

Mirren stepped in, took the mike. From the *Plymouth* she heard, "Stand by to decend."

"Hal!" she burst out. "Hal!" Then her tone went formal. "Commander Harold Paavo, a setdown at Colufo will be your death. This is Mirren Fitzgerald, Lieutenant Fitz to you, sir."

"Belay that command," the voice snapped. "About time you showed, Mirry. How's tricks? No, that's wrong. Nothing but tricks down there. You have some explainin'."

"I'll be happy to explain all day long. Home in on our radiation. But come in slow. We have native tribes and their herds. We need a little time to shoo them out of the way."

"You are speakin' freely? No guns at heads or anythin'?"

Mirren laughed in relief from tension. "Oh, Hal, it's good to hear your voice. We have had guns aplenty, but I think we are all safe now."

The Earth scout ship coasted slowly, silently, on its gravitics down out of the sky into the gompani valley. Kovas eyes, gazing upward, followed the direction as the small-eyed people finally saw the slim silvery object sliding down the air toward them. They scattered in panic, stood afar, staring.

Brian waited. He wanted to see this Hal. "Mirry," he had called her. He circled Mirren's waist with his arm as they stood side by side.

The door unlatched, the ramp slid down. Bright white uniforms strode along the slant.

"Grand reception!" Harold said, squinting through his glasses. "Didn't expect all this. Thought this planet was uninhabited by civilized locals. You people must be havin' a ball, all dressed native. Thought you might have had hardships. . . ." He waved his hand. "Good ta see you 'gain." He laid his cheek for a quick moment against Mirren's. "Lovely valley. But d'you rilly plan t'settle here in the mountains?

"Oh no," Brian injected brusquely. "This valley belongs to the Kovas. There is much empty land. Far to the southeast there will be ideal areas. You can check them out in your scout ship."

Gompani valley lay quiet. The Kovas had taken their herds away toward the grassy plains. Seasons rolled on. Great sacred fire throne mountain swirled its black rock in silence. Beams flared out from its crystals as the yann met the bright angles.

Rataq, with half a dozen Litani, flew to Colufo ahead of the Thana army. Barsorq surrendered with only token opposition. Rataq led his people to fertile fields far to the south, leaving the country around Colufo to the Thana. He offered to permit Barsorq to shuttle up to the orbiting Foqal, but he refused.

In their new location the Litani learned to be farmers and stockbreeders, planted native loggets and thalis and experimented with exotic grains such as wheat, oats, barley and rye.

In their new valleys the colonists from Earth also became farmers and stockbreeders, planting their own seeds from home and also the exotic loggets and thalis.

Both groups profited greatly from the friendly advice of the Thana. There were no zotoes; Tavita, Kors and Cogbard visited often at the ranch house of Brian and Mirren and played with their children, but they never quite understood how it could be with only one husband.

Doctor Ngora Goroga visited everywhere. She absorbed the medical knowledge of the Litani, taught it to the colony doctors from Earth. She learned the herbal lore of the Thana to carry back to both colonies. She stayed for most of the time with Rataq, but there were no children.

One new star only sailed across the night sky to Vassa. The second moved there a short time and then departed for whence it came.

In the orbiting space ship, *Foqal,* Eckem Meluq sat shrunken in his command chair, jowls sagging against the neck brace that supported his bulbous head on his flabby neck. Two F family retainers were now the total crew of the silent ship that circled Vassa endlessly—two Litani who were born on the ship, lived all their lives on the ship, had never set foot on a planet and were too fearful even to look out into space. They waited on Meluq, still calling him Eckem, swar, while his colorless eyes gazed without ceasing at the pictures called up by his flaccid fingers on the comm screen. His ceaseless mumbling had become a plaintive litany to himself about someday going down there to take command.

# SKYCLIMBER
## By Raymond Z. Gallun

PRICE: $2.25
T51682

CATEGORY:
Science
Fiction

Earth is dying, and in trying to survive, it ignores its first colony on Mars. The colonists now face certain death, and Timothy Barlow risks everything to force Earth to save the settlers. But his mission is destined to take him past Earth to the far reaches of the galaxy!

SEND TO: **TOWER BOOKS**
P.O. Box 511, Murry Hill Station
New York, N.Y. 10156-0511

PLEASE SEND ME THE FOLLOWING TITLES:

| Quantity | Book Number | Price |
|---|---|---|
|  |  |  |
|  |  |  |
|  |  |  |
|  |  |  |
|  |  |  |
|  |  |  |

IN THE EVENT THAT WE ARE OUT OF STOCK ON ANY OF YOUR SELECTIONS, PLEASE LIST ALTERNATE TITLES BELOW:

| | | |
|---|---|---|
|  |  |  |
|  |  |  |
|  |  |  |
|  |  |  |
|  | Postage/Handling I enclose ..... |  |

FOR U.S. ORDERS, add 75¢ for the first book and 25¢ for each additional book to cover cost of postage and handling. Buy five or more copies and we will pay for shipping. Sorry, no. C.O.D.'s.

FOR ORDERS SENT OUTSIDE THE U.S.A., add $1.00 for the first book and 50¢ for each additional book. PAY BY foreign draft or money order drawn on a U.S. bank, payable in U.S. ($) dollars.

☐ Please send me a free catalog.

**NAME** _____
(Please print)

**ADDRESS** _____

**CITY** _____ **STATE** _____ **ZIP** _____
Allow Four Weeks for Delivery